The Worms Shall Feast

C.R. Langille

Timber Ghost Press

The Worms Shall Feast

The Worms Shall Feast is a work of fiction. Names, places, and incidents either are products of the author's imagination or are used fictitiously. Any resemblance to actual events, locales, or persons, living or dead, is entirely coincidental.

Published by Timber Ghost Press

Printed in the United States of America

Developmental Edits by: Michael Knost

Proofreading and Line Edits by: Beverly Bernard

Cover Art and Design by: Don Noble

Interior Design: Timber Ghost Press

Print ISBN: 979-8-9925767-4-0

www.TimberGhostPress.com

Contents

This one goes out to all the trans folks out there. Keep shining in the darkness!

Chapter One

Trevor Hastings sat in the driver's seat of his '95 Toyota Tacoma that had once been black but had long-since faded to a grayish white. He had bought the truck used from the classifieds nearly ten years earlier after his parents kicked him out of the house. Although if you were to ask them, Trevor moved out to be on his own.

He had lost his virginity in the bed of the truck up Logan Canyon with his old high-school crush, Ashley Green, after running into her at Chili's one night. She was just walking out of the restaurant right as he was heading in. He didn't want to tell her he was there to apply for a job, so he lied and said he was there to grab some dinner. Amazingly, she asked if she could join him (even though she had just left) and nursed a margarita as he spent money on a dinner he couldn't afford. After eating and more than a few drinks, they headed up the canyon for a scenic drive and one thing led to another. The relationship didn't last long, but the memories tattooed his very being. Sometimes Trevor wondered if she used him. Not that it really mattered.

Seven years ago, he drove the truck up above Scofield Reservoir, where he harvested the biggest mule deer of his life. He had parked up at the top on Skyline Drive and hiked down the canyon. It was near the bottom where the old toad had decided to feed in the evening shade. The hike back out was brutal, but the truck had been waiting for him when he finally crested the top in the middle of the night with two quarters, the skull, and the hide. He drove down to retrieve the rest. Trevor didn't have the money to get the deer mounted, so he skinned and bleached the skull himself and made a damn nice European mount that was currently collecting dust in a storage unit with the rest of his belongings. And if he didn't pay the rent on that unit soon... well, Trevor didn't want to think about it.

The truck's dashboard was cracked from sun exposure, and there was a disconcerting whirring noise whenever he went above 60 miles per hour. The exterior body was dented and rusting, and it needed a tune-up he couldn't afford, but it was reliable, and it was his truck. At least for the next couple of minutes. If only the buyer would ever show up.

Trevor checked his watch as a man pulled up in a pristine, pearl-white, Audi R8. If that was the potential buyer, he was late. Hopefully, Trevor could seal this deal and get back to work before he was missed.

The man stepped out wearing a two-piece suit and a pair of Ray-Ban aviator sunglasses reflecting the afternoon sun. The man's dark hair was slicked back against his skull, a stark contrast to his pale skin. Something about his features made it hard for Trevor to determine if the man was old or middle-aged.

Something about how the man moved and presented himself made Trevor already hate the dude, but hopefully, he had the cash. Why someone who drove a car like that would want his POS truck was a mystery, but anyone who could afford that car and those clothes could easily afford Trevor's asking price. He wiped grease-stained hands on an even dirtier set of blue coveralls hoping to clean himself up a bit.

Trevor got out of the truck and waved. "Are you Randall King?"

The man smiled and took off his Aviators, revealing striking green eyes. He folded the sunglasses and put them inside the pocket of his suit. "Yes, I'm Randall. You must be Trevor."

"Yup."

Randall extended his hand. Trevor shook it and suppressed a shiver at how cold and clammy Randall's skin was. It reminded him of the wet clay he used to work with when he was going to Salt Lake Community College. Trevor was never a fan of the arts, but he needed the class to fulfill the requirements for a degree he never finished.

Randall looked past Trevor to the Tacoma. "This is the truck, yes?"

Trevor smacked the hood with his palm. "Yup! This is it. May not look like much, but let me assure you, it will take you where you need to be and then an extra mile to boot."

Randall grinned. "I like that."

Trevor smiled back, but it was forced. There was something *off* about this guy.

The grin on Randall's face never faltered as he walked around the truck and inspected the tires. When he got to the back he paused and pointed at the stickers in the window where Trevor had put a decal of some elk horns and another of a bowhunter at full draw.

"Are you a hunter?" Randall asked.

"Sure am!"

Trevor was many things, but hunting was what made him feel most like himself. From a young age, his dad had taken him bowhunting in the Utah mountains. By the time Trevor was in high school, he could out-hunt his peers and even a lot of the old-timers.

"That's great," Randall said. "So, I take it you can handle yourself in the outdoors?"

"I know my way around the forest."

Randall nodded and continued to inspect the vehicle. When he was done, he turned to Trevor. "I don't think I'll take the truck. Sorry."

Trevor's heart did a strange thing. It simultaneously dropped in disappointment and lifted with relief. He didn't want to sell the truck. He had too many memories to let it go, although he expected that it would stop working sometime very soon. That being said, he needed the money. Desperately.

"What's wrong with it? Sure, it needs a little TLC, but this thing is vintage."

"Don't get me wrong. The vehicle is fine, and I'm sure it will make a buyer happy in the future. But the truck isn't what I'm looking for." Randall pulled a card from a wallet stuffed full of cash and handed it to Trevor.

The card had a strange, disjointed spiral on the front of it placed behind the words THE LAST printed in red. On the back was a phone number.

"I represent Ms. Gwendolyn Thomas. She is producing a television show that requires skilled outdoorsmen such as yourself."

Trevor had never heard of her. He looked at the card again and then handed it back to Randall. "What does it have to do with me?"

Randall held his hand up. "Keep it."

Trevor shrugged and stuffed the card into his back pocket.

"Well, you could be on the show, Mr. Hastings."

Trevor grumbled under his breath and walked toward the driver's side door of his truck. He should have trusted his gut and driven away the moment this prick pulled up in his Audi. Here he was trying to make a living and failing horribly, yet this piece of shit, who probably hadn't missed a meal in his life, was trying to hustle him out of his hard-earned cash.

"If you don't want the truck, that's fine," he told Randall. "But don't try and bullshit me about some show that probably isn't real. Let me guess, you need some sort of deposit or processing fee from me, right? I mean, does this shit work on people?"

Randall chuckled. "Nothing like that, I assure you. The show is a reality competition. If you accept, you and several others will compete to win a prize."

Already on edge, Trevor wasn't buying it. It was still probably a bunch of crap... but you know what they say, curiosity killed the deer. He paused, one hand still on the handle of the truck's door and faced Randall again.

"What kind of prize are we talking about?"

That grin returned to Randall's face, but colder this time. "Five-hundred-thousand dollars."

"And what exactly is the competition?" Trevor asked.

"Simple. Be the last one standing. It's a survival show. We'll fly you out to a remote forest island and set you up in a spot that has everything you'll need to survive. The rest is up to you. If you tap out, you lose. Outlast everyone else, you win."

Fly out... lovely. Trevor's stomach twisted at the thought of being in the air. "Isn't there already a show like that? What makes yours different?"

"Yes, there is a similar television show. However, ours is different because you also get to take on challenges to win money. Money you get to keep regardless of whether you win the show or not."

"Like what?"

"Ms. Thomas is very interested in primitive skills and wants the show to highlight those with challenges such as making a trap and harvesting an animal with it. Building a shelter out of a certain material. Things of that nature."

Something wasn't right. Trevor had enough experience with things sounding too good to be true and ending up being a kick in the nuts.

"What's the catch?"

Randall's eyes flashed with excitement. Trevor had seen similar looks with car salesmen when a deal was almost complete. He'd seen it before when he bought his truck. The joke was on that guy though; this truck had lasted him longer than anything else he owned.

"There is no catch, Mr. Hastings. Please call the number if you're interested. We will pay you a stipend, plus provide room and board during orientation. If you don't like what you hear, you can leave and return to your normal life."

Normal life. Trevor's life wasn't normal. It was horrible.

"Think about it, Mr. Hastings."

With that, Randall returned to his car and drove away, leaving Trevor standing alone in the parking lot.

Trevor scratched his head as he tried to figure out what the hell had just happened. He got into the truck and shut the door. It was hot outside, but inside it was an oven. Not wanting to die of heatstroke, Trevor rolled the window down and sat there for a while, lost in thought. Something was up, but he couldn't quite put his finger on it.

Trevor drove back to the Quick Stop Oil Shop where he worked. As he pulled into the parking lot, a woman with a blond undercut and striking blue eyes stepped out of the garage. Geraldine was younger than Trevor, but they had hit it off from the moment she started working there. Not in a boyfriend/girlfriend kind of way; more like siblings. She had been kind enough to let him crash on her couch after his last landlord evicted him from his apartment. That had been three weeks ago.

Geraldine's arms were covered in tattoos. One side showed colorful tropical flowers, while the other side depicted a bunch of Pokémon. Her lip was pierced, and she had multiple piercings in each ear. Trevor liked that wild side of hers and secretly envied Geraldine's ability to be herself. He hated needles, and the thought of being tattooed or getting something pierced always made him shiver.

Geraldine beelined toward him. The grim look on her face let him know this wasn't going to be good. Maybe she was fed up hosting his sorry ass. He didn't blame her. This truck sale was supposed to be the windfall he needed to move out and put a deposit down on another place.

"Hey, what's up?" Trevor smiled, hoping that would ease the tension in the air, but if Geraldine wasn't her bubbly self, then whatever it was wasn't going to be good.

She leaned through the open driver's side window. "Where the hell have you been?"

Trevor glanced at his watch. It was almost three in the afternoon. "Fuck. I went to meet someone about the truck. I guess it took longer than I thought."

"Dude, longer than you thought? You've been gone over an hour!"

She was right. He had left during his break. The parking lot where he had met with Randall had only been a few blocks away. Where the hell had the time gone?

Geraldine glanced back to the shop and then turned back toward Trevor. "Mike's pissed, dude."

"Fuck. Like, how pissed?"

"Remember when Bobby forgot to tighten the lug nuts on that Corolla?"

How could he forget? The customer drove away, and when they turned the car down the street, the wheel came off. Mike was a madman that day.

"Shit," Trevor said.

"What took so long?"

"I don't know. I just started talking to this rich guy. I guess I lost track of time."

Geraldine bit her bottom lip. "Come on. Maybe if you just get back to work Mike will go easy on you."

"Maybe."

Trevor knew better though. Mike didn't go easy on anyone. If Mike could fire his own mother, he would. Besides, Mike and Trevor weren't even friends.

As soon as Trevor walked into the shop, Mike appeared out of nowhere. He was a big dude, over six feet tall. He was a linebacker in high school and kept his letterman jacket framed and on the wall of his office like it was some sort of stupid trophy, but time had not been kind. What once was muscle had long since turned soft. Trevor figured it was all the beer Mike drank.

"Well, guess who decided to show back up? I figured you had quit," Mike said.

Everyone around them continued to change oil and rotate tires, but the weight of their combined gaze was heavy on Trevor's shoulders.

"I'm sorry. I got caught up with some business during my break and lost track of time."

Mike pursed his lips and nodded, making an exaggerated frown like Robert DeNiro. "Oh, no worries, buddy."

Sirens went off in Trevor's mind. Shit... shit-shit-shittity-shit!

Mike put a hand on Trevor's shoulder and pulled him close. His fingers dug into Trevor's muscle like a hydraulic press. Maybe Mike wasn't as soft as he had thought.

"Seriously, I'll make it up to you," Trevor said. "I'll work the next two holidays or take a few extra shifts."

Mike smiled and nodded. "You don't have to do that. I mean, I don't want to take away time from your very important things. They must be important if you skipped out on work, right?"

Trevor's skin tingled as they walked. He already knew the outcome of this conversation but played along regardless, hoping that Mike was just making a show of things.

"Mike, I'm really sorry. I don't know if you know, but I was evicted from my apartment, and I'm behind on paying rent on my storage unit. I was trying to sell my truck."

Mike frowned and nodded. "Tough times for sure. Do you know what else is tough? Trying to run a business when your employees think it's okay to not be at work."

The pressure on Trevor's shoulder tightened.

"It won't happen again, I promise."

Mike stopped walking and turned toward Trevor. "I know it won't. You're fired."

Trevor's gut dropped to his knees. "Please, Mike. Come on. If I lose this job, I won't be able to find another in time to pay the storage unit."

The wrinkles in Mike's forehead deepened as he furrowed his brows.

"Well, you should have thought about that before you decided personal business was more important than your obligations. That's the problem with your generation; you don't have a work ethic. You think it is always about you. Let this be a lesson for you. In fact, let this be a lesson for all of you!" Mike's voice boomed through the small garage. "Work time is for work! Not personal shit!"

"But—"

Mike put his hand up. "No buts. Get the fuck out of here."

"Come on, Mike! Cut me some slack."

Mike shook his head and pointed to the door.

Dejected, Trevor collected his things and walked out to his truck. Geraldine watched him go and mouthed the word 'sorry.' Trevor shrugged as he left, trying to be as nonchalant as possible in front of everyone. Inside, he wanted to cry.

Mike walked out with his arms folded across his chest. That was all the signal Trevor needed. He fired up the Toyota and drove down the road.

He could sell his hunting rifle for some quick cash, or his bow. But just thinking about it made him want to throw up. Those were prized possessions. His uncle had given him the rifle when he turned sixteen, and Trevor had worked hard to earn enough money for the bow.

He slammed his fist against the steering wheel and screamed. The truck sputtered in response, and the check engine light came on.

"What now?"

Trevor pulled over into a nearby parking lot as steam and smoke began to billow from under the hood. The engine's temperature gauge was buried in the red.

He sighed and laid his head against the steering wheel. After a few minutes of feeling sorry for himself, he got out of the truck and dug his cell phone out of his pocket. Randall King's card came out with it and fell to the ground. He picked it up and stared at the number on the back of the card.

Randall picked up on the third ring.

"I am so very pleased you decided to call."

Chapter Two

Lucy Bingham sat on a log near a firepit at an unnamed campsite in the Uinta Mountains. She checked her watch for the fourth time that day and cursed. It was already forty-five minutes past when her class was supposed to start, and nobody had shown up. She stood and stretched, taking note of how her shoulders were too stiff and her legs protested the movement. Lucy would have to work on her flexibility and skip a few nights at the bar this week. Not that she could afford to go drinking. Not now.

She spied the empty logs surrounding the firepit, cursed again, and spit. She should have known better than to believe those asshat college students. The week before at Sparky's Pub, Lucy had run into a handsome man at the bar as he ordered drinks. His name was Lucas, and apparently, he was at the university studying animal conservation management. Although now she doubted everything Lucas and the others had told her. They'd promised her they would show up to her wild edible nature walk today. What a load of bullshit. She should have trusted her instincts with that group, but her positivity and hope were sometimes a weakness.

At the time, she believed them. They were nice, fun to hang out with, and Lucas had an ass that could stop a bullet. Looking back on the whole situation, Lucy was convinced they were just hanging out with her for drinks. She had spent way too much money that night, but the hopes of making it back times five by having them show up to her class was motivation enough to splurge a little. Plus, the attention was nice. Most of the attention Lucy received was rooted in ignorance or outright hate. From the way folks would stare at her in public (a mix of curiosity and/or disgust), to the anxiety she had to fight every time she used a public restroom. Being trans definitely came with its own unique set of issues. She should never have invested that much time, energy, and money in them.

Stupid.

Lucy waited two hours until she finally let herself concede the fact that nobody was coming. She let out a sigh and was packing everything up when the crunch of tires on gravel pulled her attention.

Lucy had seen students drive to her classes in all manner of vehicles, but a white Audi was a first. It looked pristine, as if it had just driven off the lot and not up a twisting dirt road.

Disappointed, she saw a man in a tailored suit emerge from the vehicle instead of one of her students. Lucy grumbled to herself and returned to packing her handouts, examples of local edible plants she had found just wandering around the campsite, and her coyote-brown backpack that contained a miniature first-aid kit, compass, knife, and some fire-making materials. The man was probably lost or one of those rich eccentric types who just enjoyed doing strange things like taking their expensive car on roads it had no business being on.

"Excuse me, but you are Miss Lucy Kathryn Bingham, correct?"

Lucy wanted to sigh, but the fact that he gendered her correctly warmed her up a little. "If you're here for the class, you just missed it." She tried to remember the last time she had given out her full name, but who knew? It wasn't like she was hiding anything.

"I see. Well, it appears it was a popular subject," the man said.

Lucy stopped and turned toward him.

He smiled at her, his eyes covered by his sunglasses.

Lucy imagined he stared at her with dead eyes, not unlike a shark. The thought made her spine tingle. He knew her, but she had no clue who he was. Lucy never liked being at a disadvantage. "I didn't catch your name."

"I never gave it," the man said with a hungry smile. "My name is Randall King, and I represent Ms. Gwendolyn Thomas."

Lucy hadn't heard of either of them. The heat combined with the no-shows made her angry and in no mood for games, so she simply shrugged. "And?"

"Ms. Thomas is producing a reality television show, and we are looking for men and women who are capable of handling themselves in the wilderness for an extended period of time with very little in the way of supplies."

She wasn't a fan of folks checking up on her and almost ended the conversation right then and there. But a reality TV show? Lucy's mind raced with the possibilities.

"Is there a prize?"

Randall lowered his sunglasses, and his emerald eyes almost shimmered in the sunlight. "Of course. If you outlast your competition, you will win a prize of $500,000 dollars. Plus, there will be plenty of opportunities to win more money by completing certain..." Randall waved his hand in the air as if he were trying to entice the word into his vocabulary. "...challenges."

Five-hundred K was a lot of money. With that kind of cash, she could stop living class to class and open a legit survival school for troubled youth like she had planned ever since she left the military.

"And you want me?" Lucy asked.

"Yes. Your outdoor survival skills are quite impressive. Besides, your skills and background piqued our interest. Two tours in Afghanistan, with a Bronze Star to boot. Quite impressive. Especially for a woman of your caliber."

Lucy's heart lurched, and her mouth went dry. They'd done their homework. Lucy didn't talk about her time in the Army much. What else did he know? Did they know about, Jeff?

"What does that mean? Who are you, really? How do you know so much about me?"

"I meant no disrespect. I simply know that your community has to fight extra hard for recognition. As for the rest, I know a lot of things." Randall's smile never faltered. He reached into his coat, pulled out a card, and handed it to Lucy.

She took it with a shaky hand. "*The Last*?"

"It's the name of the show."

Lucy wasn't one to back down from any situation or anybody. Whatever game this man was playing—and she knew from his look that he was playing something—Lucy also knew he wouldn't let up. She had met many others like him. They were dangerous. He had probably done a complete background check on her.

Lucy had her doubts. She wouldn't have made it this far in life without critical thinking, but the lure of the prize money was enough to cloud her judgement.

Randall pushed his glasses back onto his nose and headed toward the Audi.

Lucy put the card in her pocket. "I'm in."

Randall flashed that cold smile again. "I know."

With that, he got in the car and tore off back down the mountain, leaving Lucy standing there, unsure of what just transpired.

Later that night, as she sat in her bathtub soaking away the stress, Lucy couldn't stop her mind wandering. Her interaction with Randall King had made sure of that.

Lucy grew up in a tiny blip of a town in Northeastern Utah with her parents and younger brother, Jeff. To say her father was abusive would be like saying water was wet or the ducks quacked. There wasn't any room for gender non-conforming kids in the Bingham household. Just a fact of life.

Lucy and Jeff quickly learned that quiet was best, always watched to see what kind of mood their father was in when he returned from work, and had all the best hiding places pegged. Don't make a sound. Don't react. Never talk back. And don't ever cry where father could see you. It wasn't a house for pussies and faggots who wanted to wear dresses.

His words.

Lucy had spent a lot of her childhood in the back corner of her closet reading. Sometimes she'd play her Walkman loud enough that it would drown out the sound of Jeff enduring one of Father's "attitude adjustments." She always wanted to run out there and stop it. Sometimes she did and paid the price. Sometimes the fear of what would happen kept her in the closet. The shame of giving in to that fear was part of the crucible that tempered her into the woman she was today.

Lucy hated Bon Jovi, as that was the only cassette she had at the time. Those songs would sometimes haunt her at night. If she happened to catch one on the radio or at the grocery store while out and about, it would send her right back to the darkness of her closet.

Sometimes, things were fine. However, her father's violent outbursts came more and more frequently. One night, when Lucy was seventeen, she tip-toed into the kitchen to find her mother crying at the table nursing a black eye with a frozen bag of corn.

"Mom, this has got to stop. Call the cops!"

Her mother slapped her, telling her if she ever said that again, she'd tell her father. That was the exact moment Lucy realized two things: one, her mother was too far gone, and two, Lucy had to leave.

As soon as she turned eighteen, she joined the army and left home. Jeff took it the hardest. Lucy said she'd be there for him no matter what, but that she had to leave.

She wasn't there for him. Two years later, she received a phone call while deployed overseas.

Jeff was dead.

The water in the bath had turned cold. The candles had all gone out except one which did its best to illuminate the darkness and gloom. Lucy got out of the tub and patted herself dry with a big fluffy purple towel. When she looked in the mirror, her brother stared at her from the other side of the glass, a look of sadness and betrayal in his eyes as blood ran from slit wrists.

Her heart skipped a beat. She suppressed a scream and squeezed her eyes shut as tight as she could.

"Please... Go away!"

When she opened her eyes, Jeff was gone. Lucy flipped the lights on and ran into her bedroom. She opened the drawer of the cheap IKEA nightstand she bought last year and grabbed an old bottle of pills. With shaky hands, she opened the bottle and popped one into her mouth. Then, after a second thought, she took two more.

Chapter Three

Gwendolyn Thomas sat in a large, clawfoot bath that had once belonged to the Duchess of Burgundy. Warm, bubbly water that smelled of lilac and rose covered most of her body. Chopin pumped through hidden speakers, filling the room with "Minute Waltz" as she lost herself in the comfort of it all.

If the water got too cold, a snap of her fingers could have someone fix it. If the smell became too overbearing, she could have someone drain the entire tub and start over. Heaven forbid if her champagne glass went empty...

Her phone vibrated, breaking the spell and letting her know she had a message. She sat up straight and grabbed her phone, stopping just short when she saw a small patch of dry skin on her forearm. Probably just the climate.

Gwendolyn made a mental note to use more moisturizer and checked her phone. The message was from Randall.

The pieces are falling into place, just as I said they would. Just visited the last contestant. She will join us; I'm sure of it.

That brought a smile to her face. It was coming together, just like last time. Yet, this time would be different. This time, there would be a transference.

Soon, she wouldn't have to worry about stakeholders, investors, dry skin, or any of that mundane nonsense that came with life. Soon, things would be different.

Trevor opened the window shade of the jet and peered outside. A few days ago, he lost his job, now he sat in a private jet on its way to British Columbia. The plane could easily fit at least a dozen passengers. However, other than a blonde woman with an undercut coupled with a short, sleek pixie style, and tattoos up her neck sitting all the way in the back and two flight attendants, the jet was empty. He almost felt like a big damn deal.

Ten years ago, Trevor would have loved it. Flying on a luxury jet with nearly the whole cabin to himself to boot! Trevor loved planes since he was a kid. He had fond memories of his father taking him to the aerospace museum near Hill Air Force Base where they would spend hours looking at all the different types of aircraft. By the time he was ten, he knew more about planes than most adults.

It was no surprise that he got his pilot's license at an early age and seemed destined to make a career as an aviator. Trevor even contemplated joining the Air Force to be a fighter pilot. All those dreams came crashing down quite literally when he took his dad out for a flight.

Everything started out smoothly, but then the plane suffered a catastrophic engine failure. Even then, Trevor hadn't worried too much. He had practiced landing the plane with no engines. He went through the checklists, did everything he was supposed to do. But when he chose to land the plane in a nearby field—as there were no other options—the gear caught a hole in the ground he didn't see, and the plane flipped.

Trevor was okay with minor cuts and bruises. His father, not so much. He had hit his head against the window frame hard enough to lapse into a coma. First responders rushed him to the hospital, but he passed away from brain hemorrhaging two days later.

Since then, flying was no longer fun—no longer a dream. It was a nightmare.

Trevor's stomach lurched as they passed over high rocky peaks covered with snow. Staring out the window wasn't helping his nausea. He slid the cover over the window and rested his head against the wall.

The plane hit some turbulence, and Trevor grabbed the air sick bag from the back of the seat in front of him. He focused on his breathing, in, then out. In, then out. In... then his breakfast came out and filled the bag.

When he finished, he found the flight attendant standing next to him. She wore a fake smile and held out a garbage sack with gloved hands. Trevor gave her a sheepish smile as he sealed the container and tossed it in.

"Thanks," he said, though it was more of a mumble.

"Can I offer you some water? Or perhaps crackers and ginger ale?" she asked.

"Water would be fine, thank you. How much longer before we land?"

She looked at her watch. "Another hour."

The flight attendant left to get the water, and he reclined his seat, closing his eyes.

"I am so glad you decided to join our venture."

When he opened his eyes, Randall King was sitting next to him. He looked around the plane, but the only other person on board was the woman sitting at the back, as before.

"Mr. King. I, uh, I didn't know you were on board."

Randall smiled. He had a small bottle of bourbon in one hand. The flight attendant returned with a cup of coffee and a water. She handed the water to Trevor and the coffee to Randall.

"Is there anything else?" she asked.

"No thanks," Trevor said.

Randall grinned at her. "That's all for now, thank you, honey."

The flight attendant's kind face faltered for a moment. Then she regained her composure and walked back to the jet's galley.

Randall poured the bourbon into the coffee and then mixed it with a thin plastic straw. "I've been on board this whole time."

The plane shuddered as it flew through a patch of rough air. A moment later, the fasten seatbelt light lit up with an alarming ding pinging through the cabin. Trevor tightened his seatbelt and noticed Randall sported a relaxed look on his face as he drank his spiked coffee. He almost lounged in the seat, if that were possible.

"Aren't you going to fasten your seatbelt?"

Randall laughed and shook his head. "No, what's the point? We're all going to die one day. If today's the day, then a seatbelt isn't going to make a difference."

Images of crashing in the field welled up in Trevor's mind. He rubbed at his temples and took a drink of water. "That's a pretty messed up view."

"Liberating, if you ask me. Once you accept death, it doesn't have anything to hold over you anymore. Besides, death isn't always the end. Sometimes, it's an awakening to something new. Something wonderful."

Trevor swallowed hard and fought to keep his bile down. What Randall said was nonsense. It sounded like regurgitated samurai bullshit to him. There was always something you could do to try and stave death off another day.

"So, what is the island like?" Trevor asked, trying to occupy his mind with thoughts other than death.

"Open the window shade and you can see for yourself."

Trevor gave Randall an exasperated look but opened the shade. Instead of finding the rocky mountains they had just been flying over, miles of blue ocean stretched out beneath the plane. A chain of islands loomed in the distance. As the plane closed in, details came into view, showing Trevor mountainous terrain covered in pine trees.

Smaller islands led to a bigger, central island that had to be at least twenty miles from shore to shore. The jet began to descend, and Trevor spied what appeared to be a building in the center of the island.

"What is that?" he asked.

Randall didn't even look. "That is an old, abandoned mansion. More of castle, really, as it was made from giant stone bricks to simulate the fortresses of ye olden days. This island was the private getaway for Mr. Walter von Bisping. Von Bisping owned a mining company and made quite a profit."

"Who owns it now?"

"Ms. Thomas does, of course. She purchased this island from the Bisping estate many years ago."

"Does she plan to fix it up?"

"Unfortunately, no. Ms. Thomas enjoys seeing things in their natural state. In her mind, the mansion, or ruins as they stand now, is part of the island and not to be disturbed. Instead, she built on the smallest island at the end of the chain. That is where we are headed."

As the jet turned on its final leg of the descent, what Randall spoke of came into view. Nestled on the coast of the small island was a private runway, a series of hangars, a large mansion, and several outbuildings. The island itself was maybe a couple of square miles at the most. Not far from the runway was a dock with a large yacht moored, as well as three smaller boats.

"Your boss must be in the money."

"That's one way to put it," Randall said. "I'll see you on the other side."

Randall got up and walked to the front of the plane, disappearing behind a blue curtain.

Trevor focused on his breathing and congratulated himself silently for not throwing up again as they touched down. Landings gave him the most anxiety.

Once the captain turned off the fasten seatbelt light, Trevor got out of his seat. He was about to dig his carry-on out of the overhead compartment when the blonde pushed past him, almost knocking him back into the chair.

"Hey! What the fuck?" Trevor asked.

The woman looked back at him, her eyes daring him to say something or make a move. After a few heartbeats, she stormed off the plane. He watched her leave before standing back up and getting his backpack. Maybe she hated flying worse than he did. Either way, it didn't matter. He didn't come here to make friends. Trevor came here to win the prize money and change his life.

With that kind of scratch, he could quit working shit jobs and maybe make something of himself. Who knows, maybe he could even start his outfitter business and guide rich asshats into the mountains so they could kill their trophies.

Trevor walked off the plane, happy to be on the ground again. Sitting in one hangar was an expensive-looking helicopter, the same kind he saw hospitals using for life-flights. Instead of being red and white, this one was pitch black with gold stripes.

He hoped they would travel by boat to get to the big island and not by helicopter because he'd had his fill of flying for a while. In fact, he made a mental note to ask Randall if he could return to the mainland via boat instead of plane. Then he'd rent a car and drive back home.

A squat man with salt and pepper hair wearing a gray suit walked up to him. He had a clipboard in his hand and an earpiece. As he approached, he spoke to no one in particular. Trevor surmised he was on the phone with someone. Trevor pulled out his cell phone and found it had no service.

"Yes, yes, I'm walking up to him now. I'll lead him into the mansion, and you can get your first shot there. No, I don't know. I said I don't know! I have to go," the man said.

The man looked up at Trevor and smiled. "Hello, I am Wayne Danbridge. I'll be your personal assistant while you are here on Dough Island."

Trevor shook his hand and introduced himself. "Dough Island?"

"Yes, Dough Island is the island we're currently on. It is the smallest of the Pine Fern Chain. I'm the man to talk to if you need anything while you're here. Once you're on Pine Fern proper, well, I suppose you're on your own. I mean, that is the point of it all, isn't it?" Wayne laughed. It sounded forced, somewhere between a high-pitched giggle and cough.

"Yeah, I guess so."

"Great, follow me, please."

"But my gear," Trevor said and pointed to the plane.

"Don't worry. Our people will deliver your belongings to your room."

Wayne led Trevor away from the plane to a small building. A burly man stood outside the door wearing a black tactical uniform sporting a Kel-Tec KSG which was a compact, double-barreled 12-gauge shotgun capable of holding fourteen shells. Trevor had wanted one ever since they came out but never had enough money.

The guard stared at Trevor as he walked inside the building.

"What's with the security dude?" Trevor asked. "Expecting a raid?"

Wayne let out that shrill laugh again. "Oh, you know, bears and wolves."

"Right..."

As if on cue, the birds stopped chirping, and the security guard tensed and slightly raised his weapon while staring into the trees. Trevor froze, unsure if he should run or not.

A moment later, Wayne let out that same high-pitched laugh and slapped Trevor on the shoulder.

"See, bears! Come on, let's get inside so I can show you some things," Wayne said.

Trevor followed Wayne into the building. Outside, it was warm and humid, but inside the building was the wonderful world of air conditioning. Trevor didn't mind being out in the elements when he was hunting or camping. It was part of the experience. However, he never took air conditioning for granted. There really was something about a climate-controlled space. Whoever had invented it, Trevor hoped they had won many accolades.

Wayne drabbled on about how many rooms were in the mansion and how long it took to construct, but Trevor had stopped listening to him a long time ago. Instead, he stared at the art hanging on the walls.

Dozens of paintings depicting scenes of savage hunts from across the world decorated the space. One in particular showed what looked like a medieval nobleman spearing a boar. In the background, there was a giant creature in the woods watching from the shaded trees. At first, he thought maybe it was a stag or an elk, but the more he stared, the more monstrous it appeared. Its head was pale, bone-like, and the eyes...

There was something about it that made Trevor's skin crawl. He couldn't quite put his finger on it. Maybe it was the way it was hidden but also in plain sight that unnerved him. Maybe it was the way the nobleman's retinue of servants looked like they knew it was there but refused to look.

Trevor got a little closer to get a better view. The beast in the woods seemed to move in the painting, as if it were breathing. He reached out with a finger to touch the creature.

"Please don't touch that," a feminine voice said.

Trevor turned and found a tall redheaded woman with her hair in a flawless, tight bun. She stared past Trevor at the painting while smoking a cigarette. She wore a sheer white dress that left little to the imagination and heels that just looked expensive. It had to be Ms. Gwendolyn Thomas.

"I'm sorry, what?" Trevor asked.

"Don't touch that. It is priceless."

Trevor looked back at the painting and a cold pit formed in his stomach. The dark figure in the woods now clutched a tree with a bony, taloned hand. Had that been like that before? Trevor couldn't remember. He was about to ask when Wayne came around the corner.

"There you are! I lost you there for a second. Please keep up, Mr. Hastings. Ms. Thomas," Wayne said and nodded in her direction.

She nodded back before turning and walking through a set of double-doors. As Trevor watched her go, his stomach lurched, and he felt like he was going to throw up again.

"Are you okay?" Wayne asked.

"Bathroom," Trevor murmured.

Wayne's smile trembled as he pointed down the hall.

Trevor rushed away and burst into the men's room. He barely made it to the toilet before he threw up everything else in his stomach. He tried to chalk it up to airsickness, but all he could think about was the figure in the painting. The thing in the woods.

Chapter Four

Wayne led Trevor throughout the building, showing him different sections and making idle chit-chat about various facts and figures. Trevor wasn't listening, though. His mind was back at the painting, thinking about that strange figure in the woods. What was it? Had it actually moved?

Trevor didn't think so. His mind had already fed him a line about airsickness and travel fatigue messing with his brain. By the time Wayne led Trevor to his room, he already thought the whole thing was just a figment of his imagination, just the stress of the whole situation playing at his nerves.

"Here we are, the Survivor Special," Wayne said. He gave Trevor a huge grin and chuckled to himself.

"Uh, thanks," Trevor said and stepped across the threshold.

It was a nice room, though it was somewhat reminiscent of a motel. A bed, closet, and nightstand—the regular fare. Cheap paintings adorned the walls, and he was happy they were nothing more than renditions of fruit and flowers. If there had been another nature scene, Trevor knew he wouldn't get any sleep thinking the creature was watching him.

Wayne told him to call if he needed anything, dropped a business card on the nightstand, and then left. Trevor walked over to the window and opened the curtain. Not far from the house, a forest of pines and aspen spread across the island.

Trevor's mind began to machinate on the environment. He knew it would start getting cold soon and would only get colder as fall turned to winter. A good shelter would be priority to keep him out of the elements and insulate as much heat as possible, otherwise the cold would drive him to tap out. Trevor always dealt with the cold better than his father had. His father was sensitive to the chill. But Trevor could go out in the snow with just a light hoodie and outlast most of his family. His mom used to call him her little abominable snowman.

He was counting on his affinity for the cold to give him an edge; however, he didn't hold any delusions of grandeur that it would be a walk in the park. Even with his ability to deal with the temperature, it wouldn't mean much when it started to snow and it got below freezing. He also knew there would be elk and deer on the islands, but it would be difficult to get any, and if he did, he would be contending with bears, wolves, wolverines, coyotes, and cougars. This wasn't going to be easy at all, but he felt he was well prepared for the trials to come.

The phone next to his bed rang, filling the small room with a loud chirp. Trevor walked over and picked up the receiver. "Hello."

"Hello, Mr. Hastings. If you would, please join us in the dining room. Dinner will be served shortly, and there are drinks and refreshments placed for your enjoyment."

The speaker was an older man with that slight warble in his voice that elderly folk got sometimes. Trevor imagined an extremely old man with wispy white hair wearing a butler's tuxedo. The mental image made him smile.

"Sure," Trevor said.

With that, the speaker hung up. Trevor shrugged and went back to the window. A heavy-duty fence surrounded the property. He'd seen high fences before, generally on hunting ranches or certain areas out in the wilderness. They were meant to keep game animals either in or out. However, this fence was something else. It was about twelve feet high and topped with razor wire. The gate to the property had a guard tower, a spotlight, and looked more like something from a medieval castle than a modern, multi-million-dollar property. Maybe there was a T-Rex out there on the island or something.

He tried to enjoy the scenery of the forested island, but the fence and security detail of the place kept pulling him out of the moment. Trevor made a mental note to ask Wayne about the fence and everything else, but he was pretty sure the man would come back with some sort of bullshit story about bears again. You don't need a fence like that for bears.

Trevor splashed some water on his face before heading out to the dining area. He was still a bit queasy from the flight but hoped maybe some food might help settle his stomach. He didn't want to show any weakness to the other contestants, as the competition had begun now. Maybe not officially, but this was a game of mental fortitude as much as it was a game of skill.

He walked down a long hall, dimly lit, with no windows. The only source of light was low-watt backlighting coming from the frames of dozens of paintings depicting a forest that lined both walls. Nothing but trees in all the pictures. There was one painting unlike the others. Instead of a forest, this one was nearly all black—a circle, or hole, or something. Darker than anything he'd ever seen before. Beneath this painting was a gold plaque that read: *That deep dark pit that would stretch on forever to nothing and everything.* Trevor wasn't sure if it was the lighting or something else, but for a moment, he felt like he was outside.

He wasn't alone either.

Trevor turned, expecting to see someone behind him, but the hallway was empty. "Hello?"

Nobody answered. He figured it was just nerves and started back down the hallway. After a couple of steps, there came a crack, as if a twig or branch had snapped. But there weren't any twigs or branches. Not real ones anyway, just paintings.

Trevor turned around again. But just like before, there wasn't anyone else in the hallway with him.

"Hello? Is someone there?"

Another crack echoed further down the hall.

Then another. This time closer.

Then another and another as something ran towards him. He couldn't see it, but the snaps and cracks were getting closer.

Trevor took a few steps back before turning and running. From the sound of it, it would be on him in a moment. The door at the end of the hallway was almost within reach.

Something breathed on the back of his neck, and Trevor let out a scream as he burst through the door. He tripped on a rug and tumbled to the floor.

Everyone stopped talking and stared in his direction. Trevor looked around the room, breathing heavily. He pointed back to the hall. "There was something in there," he said between breaths.

Wayne let out a nervous chuckle and helped Trevor up. He then went to the door and peeked through. With a flourish, he opened it wide and let out a fake scream and pantomimed being attacked by some unknown assailant.

It cut through the tension in the room, and it wasn't long before laughter filled the gaps between nervous anxiety. Trevor looked past Wayne into the hall, but it was empty, just like before.

"See, nothing there. Let's get you something to drink. I think you need it," Wayne said.

Trevor nodded. There had been something in there, hadn't there? The more he thought about it, the crazier it sounded. Maybe he did need a drink.

A couple of soft chuckles flitted about the room, but for the most part, everyone stayed quiet. Trevor forced a smile as he tried to regain his composure. The others in the room were his competition, and he had just made a fool of himself.

"I, uh, maybe there was a rat or something," he said. It was a lie. An obvious one at that. But nobody seemed to care about what he saw or thought he saw. Trevor was a distraction and a fun one at that.

A tall man with a long black beard walked up to him and clapped him on the shoulder. He was bald and had a silver tooth that displayed prominently when he smiled. "Don't worry, brother, happens to the best of us, eh? The name's Burke. Gary Burke."

Trevor let out a nervous laugh, looked at the closed door, and then back at Burke. "Trevor."

"Nice to meet you, Trevor."

"Yeah, you too."

Burke pulled him close and noogied Trevor's head. Trevor wrenched away from the big man and massaged the area. Burke continued to smile, but it lacked warmth. It was all for show, and probably more for themselves than anyone else.

Burke turned away from Trevor and walked back to another man who stood by the refreshments table. The other man was short but stacked with muscle. He had a close haircut that reminded Trevor of the military, although the man's hair was gray, and he sported a goatee.

"Hey, Matija, I think I know who's tapping first," Burke said, loud enough for everyone to hear.

Matija looked over at Trevor, his eyes judging him. Apparently, he found Trevor lacking and turned away without so much as a change in expression.

Heat flushed through Trevor's face. He took a deep breath to compose himself just as Wayne returned with a glass full of amber liquid. "What's that?"

"Whiskey," Wayne replied.

Trevor took the glass from him and sipped. Surprisingly, it was pretty good. Much better than the cheap shit he usually drank. It didn't burn on the way down, and it left his stomach feeling warm. He hoped it would take the edge off.

"Thanks."

Wayne smiled and wandered off, leaving him alone once again. He scanned the room. Obviously, Burke and Matija were competitors. He found the woman from the plane sitting on a chair in the corner drinking a glass of dark wine. She was a competitor as well; Trevor knew it just by looking at her. There was something about how she looked sitting there, uncomfortable around all the opulence. He knew because he felt the same way.

Sure, Trevor had dreamed of being filthy, stinking, rich, but actually being in the middle of it all, he knew he was like a wasp at a picnic—unwelcome.

Across the room, another woman sat on a couch across from two men. The woman was Black and bald. It didn't take long for Trevor to overhear her name was Charlize, and she appeared genuinely happy to be a participant. Unlike the woman from the plane, she was smiling and laughing as the two buffoons across from her told some story about hunting a bear in Russia. Trevor listened to the pair for a minute, and by their accents, he guessed they were from Texas or

Georgia or something. Each wore a huge cowboy hat and snakeskin boots like they were cartoon characters.

He watched the pair for a while and saw they had similar physical features. Trevor surmised they were probably brothers. He overheard the woman call them each by name at one point. One was Hank; the other was Emmett.

"Esteemed guests, may I please have your attention?"

Trevor turned toward the voice and found Randall standing near a set of double doors at the back of the room. He wore a tuxedo that would have put James Bond to shame and sported his signature smile. When all eyes were on him, he cleared his throat and continued.

"Thank you for volunteering to be participants on, *The Last.* Your skill and mental moxie will be put to the test soon when we drop you at pre-selected sites across the island. Once dropped off, you're on your own. Tomorrow, we'll go over training on how to use the camera equipment, what's in your safety kits, and how to use the emergency communicators if you wish to tap out. There is no goal other than to be the last one left. If you are the last, then you'll win the money. Plain and simple."

Everyone started clapping. Burke, along with the Texans, let out a couple of whoops and hollers. Trevor joined in and clapped as well, but his mind wasn't in the moment. His thoughts were still in the hallway with whatever had been stalking him.

Chapter Five

There was something wrong with this place and the staff. Lucy couldn't figure it out, but her spider senses had been off the charts ever since they landed. That moment outside, when the woods went quiet, she'd been in situations like that before. Right before an ambush in Afghanistan.

One moment she was talking with her fellow soldiers, the next, quiet. She remembered it distinctly being quiet moments before the first bullets zipped past her.

Yet, it wasn't the quiet that disturbed her. It was the feeling that something not only watched her but wanted her. Wanted to devour her, crack her bones, and ingest everything that made Lucy, Lucy. It was that sensation that rocked her and had kept her on edge ever since.

Lucy sipped a glass of wine and watched the idiots around her as they boasted, laughed, and tried to flex on one another. Burke was a moron, but he had the look and feel of someone who knew his way around the wilderness. The brothers, while strong on their own, might find themselves at a disadvantage when forced to split. How they got on the show together astounded her. They showed their true colors when Emmett walked by and mumbled something about her being a DEI pick for the show or something before walking off.

Matija was a wildcard and one to keep an eye on. So was Charlize. Charlize had spent her time wandering around and talking with Burke, Matija, and the two dolt brothers. She had even come over to chat with Lucy, but Lucy had given her a look that let her know she wasn't interested in social chit-chat. Charlize put on the air of the flirt, and given that she was tall and bald, she was always at the center of attention. However, Lucy couldn't quite figure out her angle.

Yet, among all the participants, it was Trevor—who had literally burst into the room screaming—that held her interest. Theatrics aside, as what else could his dramatic entrance be, there was something about the man that bugged her. Something about the way he moved. She couldn't put her finger on it.

Once Randall came in and made his initial announcements, he raised his hands and the boisterous laughter and talking faded to silence. "Now, without further ado, may I introduce Ms. Gwendolyn Thomas." Everyone started clapping again.

Right on cue, the doors opened and revealed Ms. Thomas. She was an older woman, although the only way you could tell was if you looked closely. She wore her red hair up in a tight bun and came striding out in high heels and a white dress covered in shiny sequins. The dress appeared painted on as it hugged Ms. Thomas's body like a tailored glove, leaving nothing to the imagination.

Ms. Thomas stepped into the room and gave everyone an exquisite smile, reveling in their applause. Even Lucy found herself clapping.

After a few moments, Ms. Thomas raised her hands to quiet everyone down. "Thank you."

Her accent was thick, and Lucy wondered where she was from. Somewhere in the UK for sure. Lucy took another sip of wine and waited.

"You are all about to embark on an incredible journey, and I can't even begin to tell you just how eager and honored I am to have you all here. Each one of you has the necessary skills to win. Each one of you has the desire to win, otherwise, you wouldn't be here. The question is, which one of you has the determination to win?"

Ms. Thomas walked over to the two Texans. "Will it be one of you? I wonder what will happen if it comes down to a battle between brothers?" she asked with a sly grin. The Texans' smiles disappeared as the thought played across their faces. She ambled over to Charlize. "Or maybe it will be you? You look strong and determined."

Charlize's eyes went wide, and she readjusted her clothes nervously. Ms. Thomas left the group and walked past Burke and Matija, giving them a wink.

"It could be any of you," Ms. Thomas said as she looked Lucy in the eyes.

Her gaze made Lucy a little uncomfortable, as it was quite commanding, if not a little lustful. Lucy picked up her wine and took another drink.

Ms. Thomas spun around in a circle with her arms out wide. "Please, enjoy all that I have to offer. And once again, welcome."

Everyone clapped again, although this time it wasn't as strong. Lucy had a lot of questions, but before she could ask any, Ms. Thomas left the room. Once she departed, it was as if a weight had been lifted from Lucy's shoulders, and she let out a breath she hadn't realized she'd been holding.

Nerves. It had to be nerves. Plus, Lucy didn't like being around lots of people in new places. She much preferred being alone in the wilderness. But she'd have plenty of time for that in the coming days. Lucy was about to call it a night and retire to her room when the man who had made such a dramatic entrance wandered over to her. She checked a sigh as he approached.

He stood there by her table for a moment, staring off at the crowd. At this rate, it was going to take all night just to get a few words from him, and Lucy didn't have all night. However, she didn't have a reason to be outright rude to a stranger, even if he was the competition.

"This is all so crazy, isn't it?" Lucy asked.

He turned to look at Lucy, and the expression on his face echoed her sentiment. "Yeah, I guess," he mumbled.

Lucy offered her hand. "The name's Lucy."

Trevor stared at her hand like it was a snake before taking a deep breath and shaking it. "Sorry, I uh… I guess I'm still a little airsick or something. Trevor."

Lucy nodded, though she didn't really care. "So, where you from?"

"Utah. You?"

"Same."

"Really? Small world, eh? What part?"

Small talk like this was not her forte. She hated it. "A little piece of shit town that has no streetlights, is full of assholes, and gets too hot in the summer," she said. She took another sip of wine, contemplating whether or not to grab one more glass or just go to bed.

Trevor's face flushed. "Oh, I'm so sorry. I… I didn't mean to… It's been a strange day."

Lucy forced her smile to remain hidden. She had him on edge, and that was a good thing. "It's okay. This whole thing is out of this world."

"You can say that again," Trevor said.

The others were starting to bunch back up. The Texans crowded Charlize while Burke and Matija continued to graze the refreshments.

Maybe she could get an idea about her competitors. See what kind of people they really were if she continued to chat. Lucy decided to have more wine and signaled one of the servers by raising her nearly empty glass.

"So, obviously you know the outdoors or you wouldn't be here, but what's your story?" Lucy asked.

Trevor took a sip of his drink and grimaced as the alcohol went down his throat. "I grew up outside with my dad and brother. We spent so much time hunting and camping. It was our special thing. My dad, he used to go to the Mountain Man rendezvous, primitive skills gatherings, all that shit. Then he'd turn right around and teach us."

"Sounds nice," Lucy said. Her father never took the time to pay attention to any of his kids. At least not positive attention.

"Yeah, it was."

"Was?"

Trevor took another drink, longer this time. Either he was getting used to it or stopped caring, but he didn't give the same reaction. "Yeah, my dad, he uh, he passed."

Now it was Lucy's turn to flush. "I'm so sorry."

"Yeah, me too. Thanks." Trevor killed his drink and placed the empty glass on a nearby table. Almost immediately, one of the servers came by and snatched the glass up. "So, what's your take on everyone else?"

Lucy thought about just shrugging and keeping things to herself, but the wine made her a little chatty.

"Look over there; what do you see?" Lucy asked as she nodded to Charlize, Emmett, and Hank.

Trevor stared for a moment. "Looks like folks just enjoying free food and drink before heading out to spend god knows how long in the wilderness."

"Look closer."

Trevor's face scrunched as he watched the group. Then he turned toward Lucy and shrugged. "I don't know what I'm supposed to be looking at."

"She's feeling them out. Testing them. See how she'll touch one's shoulder before looking at the other? She's gauging their reaction."

It had taken Lucy a bit to figure it out herself, but now it was obvious. Charlize was playing a game. Trying to test the brothers' resolve and loyalty. She'd touch a shoulder or a bicep, run her fingers across a chest, but it was all a test.

And it was working. When Charlize would chat up Emmett and give him her full attention, Hank would take big shots from his glass and look away with an irritated look. When she'd do the same with Hank, Emmett would curl his hand into a fist.

"Look right there," Charlize said, pointing at Emmett.

"Holy shit! How'd you catch that."

Lucy gave him a smile. "I'm good at reading people." Lucy took one last sip from her new glass before putting it on the table next to her. Watching and observing is what kept her alive back at home and in Afghanistan.

Trevor watched the group for a bit, then watched Burke and Matija before looking back to Lucy with a look that told her he was unsure of a lot more things now. Mission accomplished.

"I think I'm going to go get some sleep. It was nice meeting you."

Lucy nodded. "It was nice to meet you too. I hope you get to feeling better."

"Thanks."

Maybe Trevor had the right idea heading back to his room. It wasn't like she was going to get too chummy with these assholes. As if to accentuate her point, one of the Texans had taken his shirt off and was flexing like some sort of teenager trying to impress his crush.

The way Charlize fake-fawned over the man was almost laughable. She played the part well enough, touching the man's shoulder, laughing at his stupid jokes, and feigning interest. But Lucy had seen that look before on other women. There was a hardness behind her eyes that gave it away. Charlize was playing an angle, and she was good at it… for the most part.

Lucy finished her wine and wandered off back toward her room. The clamor of the evening died down as soon as the door closed behind her, and she found herself in the hallway of tree paintings. This is where Trevor had mentioned hearing *something*. Sure, it was a little unnerving how if you stared at the pictures long enough, the trees seemed to crowd you. But Lucy chalked it all up to anxiety, nerves, and stress.

She walked down the hallway towards her room. At one point, it sounded like something broke a branch behind her, but she ignored the sound as best she could.

Anxiety, nerves, and stress. That is all it was.

When she got back to her room, she locked the door and sat on the bed. At least it was comfortable. Lucy stripped and took the longest, hottest shower she'd had in a very long time. She was going to take advantage of all the comforts and niceties of civilization while she could. Because in less than forty-eight hours, all those luxuries would be gone and she would have to fight, kick, and struggle for every little scrap of comfort after that point. Yet, Lucy didn't worry too much about it. She was in her element when it came to living in rough conditions. Growing up, she'd had to fight for similar things.

When she transitioned, it was mentally a challenge. Rough, tough, and determined were things she was used to, and she had an edge most of the other competitors didn't have. She was sure of it.

When things got bad, most of those machismo-fueled buffoons would throw in the towel. Meanwhile, she took solace knowing that whatever this environment could throw at her wouldn't be as tough as the darkness of her childhood or the darkness of finding who was really your friend post-transition. The darkness where her brother still waited for her.

Gwendolyn found Randall outside the building. He smoked a pipe made from a black stone she wasn't familiar with. It probably had some name like voidstone or lavatite or something equally ridiculous.

The smoke from Randall's pipe wafted to her as she strode through the moonlight toward him. It had a cloying stink to it. Bitter, with hints of sweet, but an underlying acridness to it that made her bunch her nose up in disgust.

"What is that?" she asked.

Randall let out a chuckle before taking another puff and blowing a smoke ring that was nearly perfect in shape. "Oh, just a little something to remind me of home."

A normal person would have asked where home was, but Gwendolyn didn't care about any of that. She had worked with Randall for nearly twenty years and never asked him anything personal.

"A fine batch of contestants this time around," Gwendolyn said, moving upwind from Randall's smoke.

He nodded, took another puff, then put out the bowl. "Yes, indeed. I think He Who Shall Devour the Stars will be pleased.

Gwendolyn scratched at her arm. That dry patch was getting worse and becoming quite the bother.

"Do you think we'll get a transference this time?"

"We just might," Randall said. "We just might."

Chapter Six

Trevor sat in the seat of a small, single-engine plane. He was above the clouds so when he peered out the window there was nothing but a fluffy sea of white. It was moments like this he could almost imagine he was a bird. Free, flying wherever he pleased.

Yet, there was something else in the pit of his stomach, like butterflies but worse. It made him want to throw up.

"How soon before we land?"

He knew that voice, but it had been a long time since he'd heard it. Sitting next to him was an older man, balding, with a well-kept salt and pepper beard. The man wore a patched red flannel shirt, jeans, and boots that had seen better days ten years ago. Trevor smiled as tears began to well in his eyes. "Dad?"

His father turned his head toward him, shooting Trevor that half-cocked smile that was his and nobody else's. "Well, who else would it be? Tom Brady?"

Trevor had so much he wanted to say, but the words caught in his throat.

His father placed a hand on Trevor's shoulder and smiled. "You okay, kiddo?"

Trevor still couldn't talk, so he nodded instead. They flew in silence while Trevor tried to figure out what was eating at him. Something wasn't right. Anxiety crawled up his spine, taking root and spreading through his body. It only got worse every time he glanced in his father's direction. Sweat beaded up on Trevor's forehead. He wiped it away, cringing at how clammy his skin was.

"Can you believe it?" his father asked.

"Believe what?" The words came out choked and raspy. Stomach acid rose in his throat.

"We're finally heading on that hunting trip we dreamed about for years! You and me, just like we planned!"

In the background, an alarm blared to life. Trevor looked at the instrument dashboard, but everything was reading okay. As he searched for the source, his father gave him a playful shake on the shoulder.

This time, when his father touched him, pain shot through Trevor's chest and he couldn't breathe, as if a vise grip had a hold of his lungs. That signature grin never left his dad's face, even though tears flowed freely down Trevor's cheeks. His father pulled his hand away, and it left a sticky ichor on Trevor's shirt. It was red, like blood, but also fuzzy.

The alarms were louder. A voice accompanied the sound, robotic. It kept saying something, but Trevor couldn't make it out. The vise in his chest tightened, and Trevor started to panic. He looked over at his father and immediately wished he hadn't. The man's body was a broken and bloody mess. He turned his head towards Trevor, and it lolled at an odd angle as a bit of jagged bone poked underneath the skin of his neck. "What is it, kiddo?" His father's voice was wet.

A feeling of weightlessness took over Trevor's body, and he looked out the windshield of the small plane to see the earth rushing towards him.

The alarm came into focus, and so did the voice.

ALTITUDE! ALTITUDE! ALTITUDE!

Trevor woke covered in sweat and screaming. He wasn't on a plane but rather in his small room. It took him a few moments to gather himself and calm down; it had been too real. Trevor hadn't had a dream like that in many years. He tried to play it off as nerves, or maybe the flight over kicking up bad memories of what had happened, but there was something deep down inside that told him it was more than that.

When he finally got up, his shoulder and chest ached. The doctors at the hospital said Trevor was lucky to have survived the crash, unlike his father.

He got dressed, brushed his teeth, and then looked out the window. At the perimeter, a small team of men dressed in yellow jumpsuits that covered their entire bodies walked along the fence line. Two of them carried metal backpacks and held what appeared to be some sort of rifle. A long tube connected the weapon to the pack. At one point, the group stopped, and someone who looked like they were in charge pointed to a spot. The two men carrying the backpacks moved closer, and a second later, flames spewed out, scorching the ground.

"Flamethrowers..." Trevor mumbled. "What in the fuck have I gotten myself into?"

Why the hell would they need flamethrowers? What were they burning? He supposed it could be some sort of noxious or invasive weeds, but flamethrowers seemed like overkill. Ever the curious one, Trevor wanted to see for himself.

Outside of the huge building, the air was fresh and crisp. Birds chirped nearby and morning dew covered nearly everything. He oriented himself to where the team had been and started toward the fence. The men were long gone by the time he got there, as well as any evidence of what they had incinerated. At Trevor's feet was a blackened and scorched patch of earth.

He walked up and down the fence a bit to see if he could find anything that would help him figure out what it was, but other than a couple more burnt patches, there was nothing. He made a mental note to ask about it.

On his way back, Trevor came across Charlize. She sat cross-legged in the grass with her eyes closed and her hands in her lap. He watched her for a moment before realizing she was meditating. Trevor didn't want to bother her, so he turned to go the other direction.

"It's nice out here, isn't it?" Charlize said.

Trevor turned back and found her with her eyes open. She cast a smile in his direction, and he could tell why the others fawned over her last night. Charlize was stunning, a sight to behold, and her charismatic aura was almost overwhelming.

"Uh, yeah, I suppose."

Charlize patted the ground next to her. "Come join me."

"Oh, I'm not into all that," Trevor said and waved his hand around in a circle accentuating *all that*.

Charlize laughed and her smile grew bigger. "No silly, not to meditate. To chat."

Trevor's face flushed with heat. He hesitated until she patted the ground again and then found himself walking over without thinking about it. He sat down next to her. The grass was damp and cool to the touch.

"So, where you from?" Charlize asked.

"Utah. You?"

"Washington, not too far from Spokane. I live with my mom and sister in a patch of ground that the family has owned for generations. My great-great-grandpa homesteaded it back in the day."

"That's awesome. I'd love to own land one day. Maybe if I win this thing I can buy a good plot somewhere."

Charlize nodded, but her smile faded ever so slightly.

Trevor, unsure of what to say next, blurted the first thing that came to his mind. "What will you do if you win?" he asked.

"My sister is sick. They say she needs a new kidney, and soon. So, if I win, I'll use the money to pay those pesky little hospital bills." Charlize had tried to say it with a chipper attitude, but there was ice beneath her warmth.

"I'm sorry to hear that. What about insurance?"

Charlize looked off into the horizon. "It's complicated."

Trevor knew that waltz all too well. He nodded. "Yeah, I hear you," he said, glancing at his watch.

Charlize wiped her eyes. "So, is that why you're here too? Money?"

It was Trevor's turn to look away. That was exactly why he was here, but being broke and needing money to pay for a sibling's organ transplant were two different animals. He didn't want to admit he was just in it for the money. "Don't get me wrong, the money would be wonderful. But I'm doing it to prove myself, to show my dad that I can do something like this and stick with it."

Charlize pursed her lips before cracking another genuine smile. "I'm sure your dad will be proud of you regardless of whether you win or not."

Maybe. Too bad he wouldn't be around to see it either way. "Yeah," Trevor said.

He glanced again at his watch. "We better get to the orientation. It's going to start soon."

"Okay. I'll meet you there," Charlize said. "I just want to take in the scenery a little longer."

"Okay, see you."

Trevor got up and walked away. He felt stupid for lying about why he was here. Why did he need to lie? Money was money, and everyone needed some. Some more than others. And what was that crap about proving himself to his dad? Maybe it was a suppressed feeling he had or something. Maybe he needed therapy like his mom insisted. Maybe... or maybe he just didn't know how to be extroverted.

Trevor slowly made his way to the orientation meeting. It was a crisp morning, a portent of what was to come, but for the most part, Trevor tried to enjoy the scenery. However, something about the whole situation didn't sit right with him. In fact, he seriously considered asking if he could still back out. Perhaps he would go through orientation and see how he felt after.

Trevor turned the corner and found everyone gathered out in the courtyard. Several canopy tents covered tables of food and drink as well as a row of chairs facing a small stage and podium with a large projector screen set up.

The strong aroma of coffee hit Trevor's nose, and he smiled. That was exactly what he needed. He poured himself a cup, added a bit of sugar, and then grabbed a particularly yummy-looking cream cheese danish before taking a seat.

Emmett and Hank sat together laughing about some inside joke involving a cow and a badger or something. Emmett nodded hello as Trevor came over. Trevor mumbled a greeting, but his mouth was already full of the danish.

"So, you ready to do this thing?" Hank asked.

Trevor swallowed his pastry and shrugged. "Yeah, I think so. You?"

Lies. He wasn't ready at all.

"Emmett and I were born ready. Isn't that right, Brochacho?" Hank said, slapping his brother on the shoulder. "You might as well save yourself the weeks of starving and just back out now."

Hank laughed, though his eyes didn't reflect the same glimmer as his smile. Trevor considered asking why they had entered the competition but decided against it. In the end, he really didn't want to know why everyone had shown up. It would only eat at his conscience in the inevitable days of solitude to come. Plus, he didn't really care for the brothers. Their alpha male bravado was annoying at best.

The two brothers started bullshitting again, and Trevor glanced over to the food table, halfway considering eating another Danish. Hell, this was probably the last decent meal he would have for the foreseeable future.

Burke and Matija stood next to the food, loading up plates. Matija was telling Burke about how his grandma used to make the best breakfasts. Burke wore dark sunglasses and kept silent. Trevor knew that look, even behind the sunglasses. Burke was hungover. Not the best way to start a survival competition.

"Hey, maybe a little hair of the dog might help," Trevor said.

Burke turned to look at him, his gaze heavy even behind the sunglasses. A moment later, Charlize arrived. She wore a bright expression and had thrown on a woolen hoodie but still wore her yoga pants from before. After grabbing a glass of orange juice and a plate of fruit, she went and sat by Hank and Emmett.

Lucy sat by herself in one of the far chairs, picking at a plate of bacon and eggs. She wore the same look as she had when they first arrived—one that said stay the hell away from me. Trevor thought about going to sit by her but decided to give her space.

He glanced at his watch and noticed it was time to get started. As if on cue, Randall walked up to the podium. He no longer sported his fine business suit. Instead, he wore a pair of jeans, a blue flannel shirt, and a puffy vest. Somehow, he made the outfit look like it was worth more than a month of Trevor's pay.

Everyone took a seat as Randall watched them from the stage.

"Thank you, one and all. Today, we are going to go over a lot of information, so please, pay attention, and don't be afraid to ask any questions," Randall said.

The man's voice was loud. Trevor looked around but couldn't see any speakers.

"Tomorrow morning, we will fly you to your drop locations. We have split the island up into different zones and assigned one to each of you at random. These areas have all been pre-scouted and contain everything you will need to get you started."

Randall pointed to the screen. An image of the island popped up with superimposed lines showing it had been sliced up evenly for the contestants. The center of the island looked like it held a crater lake. Trevor strained to see more, as it appeared there was some sort of structure in the middle of the lake. He raised his hand.

"Yes, Mr. Hastings?" Randall asked.

"Is that the von Bisping estate?" Trevor asked.

"Very perceptive, Mr. Hastings. Yes, indeed it is. However, it is very dangerous, as it has fallen to the elements. The center of the island is off limits. In fact, you are not to venture outside of your zones during this competition. If you do, you will be disqualified."

"Why is that?" Emmett asked.

"This is about surviving on your own. We've seen in the past that contestants can act outside of their normal character when put into a stressful situation and knowing their neighbor may have more resources than they do. Therefore, this rule is very strict and cannot be broken under any circumstances. Do we all understand this?"

Everyone nodded.

"Excellent. The next thing I would like to talk about are the personal challenges." Randall held up a purple envelope with gold filigree. "If any of you find one of these in your camp, it's your lucky day. These are the personal challenges. If you complete the challenge, you will earn the money attached to said challenge regardless of whether or not you win the show."

Lucy raised her hand. Randall nodded in her direction. "Yes, you have a question?"

Lucy cleared her throat before continuing. "Who is going to deliver the challenges? Do you have personnel on the island itself?"

"Great question," Randall said. "Maybe we do, maybe we don't. Perhaps it is a drone? Either way, you will never see how we deliver them, as that is a trade secret."

"Trade secret? I bet it's just your staff out in the woods or something," Burke said.

"Maybe. Regardless of how they get delivered, consider yourself lucky if you receive one. Any other questions?"

"How will you know if we complete the challenge? Are we supposed to record it with the cameras?" Trevor asked.

"Another great question. Yes, record it with your cameras, but don't worry if you don't capture it all or it doesn't turn out great. We have hidden cameras and overhead imagery that will help put your story together when the time comes."

Overhead imagery? How did they swing that? Trevor tried to think if just anyone could launch a satellite into space with a camera on it when Randall continued to speak.

"Later today, one of our local survival experts will go over some of the poisonous plants to avoid on the island, and we will do a final inspection on your gear to ensure you only have approved items. You will also get plenty of hands-on training with the camera equipment and emergency communications equipment. We'll go over check-in schedules, when the medical team will come, and what they will look for during their visits. All your questions will be answered. After that, you will be left to your own devices to prepare."

The rest of the day went by quickly. Trevor listened to everything Randall and his team had to say, but he couldn't shake the feeling that he should back out, go home, and put all this behind him. In the end, he convinced himself it was only nerves and that things would get better once he was out in the woods.

Randall sat at his desk. He had each of the survivalists' files out in front of him. Their team had done well picking contestants this time around. It would be easy to make them disappear. To make things look like an accident.

Gwendolyn walked into his office without knocking, causing him to flinch when the door opened unexpectedly. She was a petulant child but served her purpose well. Hopefully, this would be the last season, and he could be done with all of this.

"Everything is ready for tomorrow?" she asked.

"I've taken care of it all."

"Excellent. Do you think any of them suspect?"

Trevor perhaps, but the boy didn't seem to know enough to put the dots together. "No. I don't believe any of them are aware of what is waiting for them on that island," Randall said.

"Good. It's better that way."

Indeed, it was better that way. But they'd find out soon enough.

Chapter Seven

Lucy sat in the back of the small helicopter as it skimmed through the air only a few hundred feet off the water. She had not gotten much sleep the night before, mainly due to nerves. Scenarios and ideas had raced circles in her mind as she went over what she needed to do once they dropped her off in her spot. Aside from that, she couldn't sleep well because the ghost of her dead brother kept watching her from behind the dresser, blood still caked his hair. He didn't say anything this time but stared at her with a horrified expression.

At one point, she covered her head with the blankets to try and block him out, but that only made him angry. Lucy swore she could feel him tugging at the blankets.

Was it real? Or was it her brain trying to process the trauma of her childhood like the therapist had told her? Lucy had no idea anymore, but it didn't matter. It was real enough to keep her awake.

All that said, she wasn't too tired, as anticipation buzzed in her chest. All that latent energy made her tap her foot on the floor of the helicopter as if she were trying to send a message in Morse code.

The island itself was beautiful. It would be her home for the next few months at least. Lucy was determined to make it to the end and be the last. She just had to play it smart and not overexert herself, make stupid decisions, or get injured.

Lucy was the third one out after Hank and Emmett. They took each contestant out separately so that nobody would get an unfair advantage or see exactly where the others were located. She preferred it this way. If they had all been together, she would have had to listen to them ramble on and boast.

Finally, the helicopter turned toward land. Lucy immediately started scouting the best she could while they were still in the air, assuming this was to be her spot. She tried to remember the map of the locations to get an idea of her area. If she was correct, this area had a small year-round stream that cut through the middle of the zone and emptied into the ocean.

The pilot found a flat spot and landed. One of the security guards, a burly man with a beard and a nose ring, got out with his shotgun first. He scanned the area before motioning Lucy to exit the aircraft.

She still didn't quite understand the need for these guards, but who knows, maybe bears were a bigger issue than she thought. Lucy grabbed her pack and hopped out, keeping her head low.

The guard nodded to her but kept scanning the distance with the shotgun clutched in his hands. He backed back up to the helicopter and climbed in just before it lifted into the air and sped away.

Lucy watched the helicopter until it was out of sight and she couldn't hear the blades beating the air to stay aloft. Then, she turned and surveyed her zone.

The ocean waves lapped at the shore, which was covered in good-sized rocks. She made a mental note to be careful traversing the area, as those rocks were sure to be slippery, and she could snap an ankle easily.

Not too far up the beach inland was the tree line made up of fir, alder, and cedar. Lucy took a moment to soak it all in. The waves were rhythmic, and a breeze blew past, moving the trees and letting them sing and groan.

She would have loved to sit there for hours and simply bathe in the sunlight listening to the island's song. There would be plenty of time for that later. For now, she needed to get a better idea of her new home. Besides, it wouldn't be too long before the refreshing coziness of it all took a turn. Surviving wasn't fun. If you were having fun, it was camping. She knew that soon the cold would creep in, sapping the warmth and energy from her body. Depending on what she could find to eat, the hunger would set in, and each action would become a game of give and take to try and figure out if the calorie expenditure would be worth it or not. No, a world of hurt and suffering was coming her way, but hopefully, at the end of that tunnel would be a fat paycheck.

Lucy walked down the beach for a bit and then cheered when she came to the stream. It was in the location she thought it was. She followed the stream inland and found what looked like old huckleberries and even a few Oregon grape plants with blue berries. The huckleberries were dry but edible, though it would be a few weeks before the grapes would ripen. However, Lucy took their presence as a good sign and a source of food.

Oregon grapes were an excellent source of vitamin C, and she could probably make tea out of the huckleberries. There weren't a lot, but hopefully, she would find more once she really started exploring. Her priority was to find a decent spot to get started on her temporary shelter.

Lucy planned to make a temporary shelter first, just to have somewhere to sleep, and then get to work on a more permanent structure after. Her idea was that the temporary one would provide warmth and keep her out of the elements—which was a heavy priority—and then she could take her time with the better shelter, which would hopefully mean fewer screwups. It was a gamble, because if the weather turned sooner than anticipated, she'd be scrambling to get something put together.

She hiked upstream another hundred yards or so before she came to an area that didn't have any widow makers. She knew from experience that dead trees or heavy broken limbs could come down at any moment and didn't care if you were awake or asleep. Getting hit by one of those in the middle of the night could injure a person or possibly kill them. Hence the name, widow makers.

The spot was close to the stream, so she would have plenty of water, and from her camp she had a view of several game trails, which would be great for setting snares or even harvesting a deer or moose.

Lucy made one more pass through the area to make sure there weren't any poisonous or toxic plants. During her search, she spotted several orange-yellow, trumpet-shaped mushrooms that looked like chanterelles next to some old growth evergreens. Safety first. She wanted to make sure they were what she thought they were.

Lucy suppressed her excitement as best she could as she dropped to her knees and cut one of the mushrooms away. The cap was wavy, and the underside had wrinkles more so than gills. As a final test, she broke it apart revealing a white interior.

"Oh, hell yeah!"

They were chanterelle mushrooms! What an amazing and fortuitous find! Lucy searched around and found even more of the fungal delights. She was so excited that she temporarily forgot about what she was doing. Instead of searching for toxic plants, Lucy kept looking for more mushrooms. All in all, she found at least six spots within 300 yards that held the chanterelles.

As she kept looking around the fir trees, she pulled away some of the undergrowth and found a different kind of plant. At first, she thought it was some kind of lichen or moss like Old Man's Beard. It was clumped up and stringy at the base of a tree. However, instead of the light green or white she was used to, this moss was blood red. It looked dried out despite the wet weather of the region.

Lucy reached out to touch it but stopped herself at the last moment. Having never encountered this type of moss before, she had no idea if it was toxic or not. Plus, nearby were the bones of what looked like an old rabbit kill.

Lucy decided to leave the moss alone and got back to task. For her temporary home, she opted for a lean-to debris shelter. It would be easy to make, keep her warm enough, and wouldn't take a ton of energy expenditure. There was a fallen pine in the area that would provide an excellent backbone or wall. She quickly gathered a bunch of fallen limbs and laid them upon the fallen pine at a 45-degree angle. Then, using some paracord, she lashed them together and tied her tarp to the top of it, laying it across the limbs like a blanket.

Lucy gathered some good-sized rocks and placed them at the bottom and the corners of the tarp before layering pine boughs on top of that to add more insulation and protection from the elements.

She didn't rush the shelter, as she didn't want to burn unnecessary calories. By the time she was done, it was midday, and her stomach growled. Lucy grabbed some of the nearby huckleberries and the one chanterelle she had picked and ate those while sitting by the stream. She realized she would need water, which would mean she needed a fire to purify the water.

Lucy gathered some stones to make a firepit near her shelter. Later, she would build a wooden fence next to the fire to act as a heat reflector, but for now, she just needed to keep it simple.

After making the pit, she found some kindling and prepared some of the leftover limbs from her shelter project for the fire by cutting them to size. Then, using her ferro rod, Lucy used the steel striker, and amazingly, the nest of kindling she made caught on the first try. It started to smoke, so Lucy grabbed the bundle and brought it up to her face before gently blowing into it. The smoke became stronger, so she felt confident enough to start swaying the bundle through the air, providing even more oxygen. A moment later, it burst into flames.

With a good burn, Lucy put the nest into the firepit where she had placed the limbs. It wasn't too much longer before she had a strong fire going. Lucy was happy they let the contestants bring ferro rods. Trying to start a fire using friction or a different primitive method would have been very difficult. She knew how, and she was skilled at it, but she also knew that sometimes skill didn't guarantee a fire, or that it could take her hours or even days to get one going.

Once the fire was lit, she gathered some water from the stream in her pot to get it boiling so she could use it for drinking. It was nearly the time she needed to take her HRT, and she'd need some water to swallow the pills.

The contestants were allowed enough personal medication to last ninety days with the promise that if the competition was still ongoing after that, the production team would provide them with refills.

Not wanting to let the fire burn out, Lucy went to gather more wood. She took the opportunity to search out in a different direction across from the stream.

The trees began to thin out a little, and soon she found herself in a tiny meadow. It was quite picturesque and could be another good spot for her permanent shelter. However, sitting in the middle of the meadow on its side was the desiccated remains of a bull moose.

Lucy dropped her gathered wood and went to examine the animal. It was mainly bones, though some of its hide stretched across the skull and ribs like a mummy's wrapping. It didn't smell too bad, and given the condition of the remains, she figured it had died earlier in the year or maybe even late last year.

There were supposed to be bears, mountain lions, and wolves on the island, so finding a dead moose wouldn't be out of the ordinary. However, there was something off with it. Even though it was old, it didn't look like it had been taken down by a bear or anything of the sort. Its ribs were cracked open as if something had hit it hard to get to the insides.

More of that old red moss she had found earlier had grown all around and even inside the dead animal. Yet, there was still something else that made her uneasy. Something that made her back away slowly and gather up her wood to return to camp.

The moose's skull appeared to have been crushed in by a rock or something similar. A quick search revealed the weapon itself—a large rock with a pointed end, stained with a rusty brown.

Chapter Eight

Trevor held an arm across his face to protect it from flying debris as the helicopter took off, hovered for a moment, and then turned. He watched it fly away until the rhythmic beat of the rotor blades became nothing more than a whisper in the distance.

As soon as it was gone, it was like a gentle wave of relaxation radiated through his body. He didn't have to worry about the weird paintings in the halls or what the security teams were scorching. Now, Trevor had a task, and while it was harder than it sounded, it was straightforward. He had to outlast the others and survive.

The shore was a little rocky, but for the most part, it was just sand and dirt. Not too far from the beach, tall pines reached towards the sky, a bulwark or border warning others to stay away. The wilderness was like a second home to him. He had spent so much time hunting and camping with his father that he felt... No, he didn't want to jinx it.

Trevor grabbed his gear and dragged it up past the shoreline, leaning his pack against a nearby tree. In the distance, the mountains shot up into steep, craggy peaks. He wished he had paid more attention during the orientation. Randall and his team had presented them with a map of the island and all the contestants' zones. Maybe if he hadn't had been so preoccupied with his inner turmoil, he would have a better idea of what was nearby.

It was too late now. First things first, he needed to find some fresh water. Trevor knew that all the zones had water, so he wasn't too worried. Though the mind had a funny way of messing with you. The moment he thought about finding water, he became thirsty. It was ridiculous. He had a bottle of fresh water from the main island in his pack, and he knew he'd find some in his zone before too long.

He searched around for a bit, coming across some small game trails and areas that looked decent for snares. Hell, he even found some fresh deer sign and made a mental note to hunt the area later. If he could bag a deer or elk, it would be a game-changer and put him in a good position to win this thing.

He had brought his recurve bow along just for such an occasion. They allowed him to also have ten arrows. To the average Joe, that may have sounded like a lot of arrows, but he knew from experience that they could easily break or get lost.

After a little more searching, he found a small creek that fed into a pond. From the looks of the tracks on the ground, a variety of deer, elk, and even moose used the pond as a watering hole. He even found some cougar tracks.

That gave him a bit of a pause, though cougars rarely messed with people... mostly. However, if he did harvest an animal, Trevor decided he would process it away from his camp. If he lasted into the winter months, the food would definitely attract predators.

Not too far from the creek, Trevor found a crevice set into a section of hillside that started to rise in elevation. The opening was narrow but large enough he could walk through. Once through there, the crevice opened into a larger area. The top was exposed to the open air, but it gave him an idea. He could turn this into his shelter. If he built a fireplace with a chimney to let the smoke out, then built a roof made from timber to keep him safe from the elements, the natural formation of it all would keep him warm. Especially if he lined the wall with stones to retain the heat from his fire. It would be a lot of work but once completed it would be a solid shelter.

The sun had risen even higher into the sky, causing Trevor to glance at his watch. He couldn't believe it was almost midday already. It felt like only moments since the helicopter had taken off, but three hours had passed.

He gathered his things and brought them up to the crevice. Next, Trevor gathered a bunch of wood for a fire. His father had taught him to take his time with preparing a fire, saying more time in prep means less time trying to coax a flame to life. It was something Trevor had taken to heart, so over the next thirty minutes, he prepared the wood by cutting larger chunks into smaller chunks and separating all the different sizes into piles. He prepared his kindling and had been lucky enough to find an empty bird's nest that had fallen from a tree. Trevor used that to get the fire going. A few quick strikes from his ferro rod and the nest caught.

With everything ready to go, it wasn't long before he had a strong, healthy fire. He gathered some water from the pond and boiled it in a pot he had brought.

The next part was going to be labor intensive. Trevor started gathering rocks and piling them up next to the crevice. After he got everything he could nearby, he started making trips to the beach and back. He took care not to get overworked, but he still ended up sweating. Burning all these calories might bite him down the road, but Trevor figured he should probably use what energy he had now, as it would just be harder the longer the contest continued.

Deciding to take a break and cool down, Trevor drank some of the purified pond water. It wasn't the best tasting, but it would keep him from getting dehydrated. While he rested from hauling rocks, he got to work cleaning the crevice out of excess debris.

He used a large piece of bark as a shovel and found a decent branch from a nearby pine to use as a broom. The back of the crevice had collected a lot of dead leaves from the nearby aspens, but the broom and bark made short order of them all. As he cleared the last of the leaves, he uncovered a rock with some carvings on it.

The carvings looked like hash marks in sets of five, like someone had kept tally. Perhaps this spot had been the home of a previous contestant. He reached down and lifted the rock, revealing a hole in the ground with a small, plastic weatherproof box inside it. It was the same kind of box Randall's people issued him to store batteries for his camera equipment.

Trevor grabbed the box and headed back out near his fire. He sat on a nearby log and flipped the latches, opening the box. The hinges squealed in protest, but they opened easily enough. What he found inside only further confused him.

Inside the box were several IDs. The top one belonged to a middle-aged man with blonde hair and green eyes. His name was Jimmy Haskin, and apparently, he lived in Ohio. The next one was a woman with thick glasses and ruddy complexion named Rachel who lived in Alaska. This one had a bloody fingerprint stain on the back. There were five others in the box too, various folks from different parts of the world.

Trevor put everything back into the box and closed it up. It had to be a past team of contestants or something of the sort. But why were they hidden under the rock? Trevor decided he would ask about them when the medical team came for their first check. However, regret and doubt had started to grip his mind. Something was off; he just couldn't tell what.

The click of Ms. Gwendolyn Thomas's designer heels echoed down the hallway. It gave her a small modicum of pleasure to know that the little peons in the operations room would hear her coming and were no doubt scrambling around like ants in an effort to look busy.

She paused just outside the metal double doors and pressed her thumb against the fingerprint reader. The red light next to the reader flashed green, and a quiet click let her know the door had unlocked.

She pushed through the doors and stepped into the room. Just as she had expected, a half-dozen men and women in white button-up shirts and ties were all pretending to appear hard at work. She even caught one of them turning a whiteboard around in a hurry. More than likely, it was an odds board, and they were taking bets.

Of course, Gwendolyn knew there wasn't much to monitor on the first day of the competition. Yet, she still expected them to stay on task. Gwendolyn scratched at her arm. That bloody rash was worse, and they were hundreds of miles away from the nearest doctor. It could wait though. There were more important things to worry about.

"Status report," she said to nobody in particular.

A few of the techs looked at one another, but nobody made a move to say anything. They all avoided her gaze. Gwendolyn was about to get angry when the door to the back office opened and Randall stepped out. He held a cup of coffee in one hand and sauntered over to her. The techs took the opportunity to get back to work.

He took his bloody time and even had the audacity to take a sip from his mug before smiling at her. She admired his power and influence, but the moment those ran out, she would hang him out to dry like everyone else. People were tools to be used, nothing more.

"Well?" she asked, putting a hand on her hip.

"Everything is going smoothly," Randall replied. He took another sip of coffee, sighed with pleasure, and then held the mug up to his face. "Quite an amazing thing, really. People can be quite ingenious when they want to be."

Gwendolyn stared at him as the impatience ate at her insides. "The status report?"

"All the subjects are in their quadrants, busy at work setting up their shelters or trying to gather food. You should watch some of them." Randall turned towards one of the big screens on the wall and pointed.

The monitor showed an aerial view of the island in real-time. Randall walked over to one of the techs, a large, bearded man with a face full of freckles, and placed a hand on the man's shoulder.

"Zoom in, please. Let's show Ms. Thomas what is happening here," Randall said.

Freckles audibly swallowed and punched a few commands into his keyboard. A moment later, the video zoomed in until it showed Burke hard at work using a handsaw to cut down dead pine trees. Nearby, a pile of half a dozen long lodgepole pines lay on the ground.

"See, busy little ants," Randall said.

"Yes, very interesting. Do any of them suspect anything?" Gwendolyn asked. She couldn't care less what the subjects were doing to prepare for surviving.

"Not at all."

"And what about Him?"

Randall nodded at Freckles once again. The man entered a new command, and the feed on the monitor changed. It showed a dark room with a dirt floor. The room itself wasn't well lit, but the camera switched automatically into night vision mode, picking up all the light it could, allowing her to see a little better. Dozens of bones from various animals were strewn about the floor with reckless abandon. There was even a human skull lying on its side in the corner. Sitting in the opposite corner of the room was a large mass, curled up and sleeping. It breathed deeply with big shuddering gasps. Red moss grew from where the creature slept and had made its way up one wall and across half of the floor.

"Still sleeping, though he has begun to move and should be waking soon. The stars are moving to their proper alignment," Randall said.

"Excellent. Notify me when He is awake."

"Of course," Randall said and took another sip of his coffee. "So good. I will miss some things."

Gwendolyn rolled her eyes and left the operations room. Things were going as planned, and soon it would begin in earnest.

As she was about to leave, she saw Freckles standing nearby. The man held a clipboard like it was a shield.

"Can I help you?" Gwendolyn asked, trying to channel as much rhetorical energy as she could muster into her tone.

"Uh, yeah. Just a question. Like, is what we're doing helping keep the rest of humanity safe?"

The question took Gwendolyn by surprise. Keep the rest of humanity safe? What was it they thought they were doing here? What did Randall tell these poor idiots?

Before she could answer, Randall stepped up and put a hand on Freckles' shoulder. "Of course, we're keeping the rest of humanity safe. Just think what kind of damage and destruction He would cause if he got to the mainland."

The doubt still lingered in Freckles' eyes, but Gwendolyn could tell Randall had already gotten his foot in the door. Watching him manipulate people was quite entertaining. Gwendolyn smiled at it, and Freckles must have taken that as her agreeing with Randall.

"Right, but these people are going to die," Freckles said.

"Sacrifice a few to save the many," Randall said. "Besides, these people aren't good people. Matija is a wanted criminal in three countries."

Freckles looked at his feet. "Yeah, I guess. But—"

"No more questions. We are keeping the world safer by doing this, rest assured. Now, get back to work."

Freckles nodded and shuffled off. Gwendolyn would have thought the amount they paid the techs would keep the questions at bay, but apparently not. She made a mental note to have Randall vet the help better for the next go-around. As she left the operations room, she couldn't help but scratch at her arm.

Chapter Nine

The thrum of the single-prop engine was almost more of a feeling than a sound. It was a feeling Trevor had come to love because it meant he was flying. Something was amiss, something that Trevor couldn't quite pinpoint. He checked the instrument panel. His altitude was good. He was flying in the right direction. Airspeed, fuel levels... it was all how it should have been. But his gut told him something was wrong.

It all felt too familiar.

"What's up, kiddo?"

Trevor's heart dropped at his father's voice. He was afraid to look, as memories of that day came crashing back to him. His father shouldn't be here. Trevor shouldn't be here. But he couldn't help himself and glanced over at his dad. His father wore the same outfit as the last time, red flannel and jeans. This time, he had a concerned expression on his wrinkled face, accentuated by his gray, bushy eyebrows.

"I-I don't know. Everything seems fine, but..."

His father smiled. "Probably just getting excited for the trip."

"Yeah, I guess so."

But that wasn't it. This wasn't excitement or nerves. It was something else. Trevor looked out the window. They were 5000 feet above the water.

There shouldn't be water. Not like this. There should be mountains.

"Well, now you've gone and done it," his father said, his voice gruff, tinged with anger and frustration.

Trevor looked away, catching smoke coming from his dad's shirt. The stink of singed flesh and burning hair filled the cabin. It took everything he had to keep his eyes on the instruments.

"Look at me, kiddo."

Trevor slammed his eyes shut and shook his head. "No. This isn't real."

"But it is real. You killed me."

"No! It was an accident. I..."

"Nothing but excuses. Just like that whore mother of yours!" His father's voice boomed inside his headset.

Trevor took the green Dave Clark headphones off and threw them behind him. He kept his eyes closed, afraid of what he would see.

His father grabbed his wrist and squeezed. Trevor let out a yelp as the bones in his wrist cracked under the pressure.

"Look and see."

Trevor opened his eyes. His father was nothing more than a desiccated husk in the passenger seat. Red moss with strange blooming plants grew out from the corpse and had taken over most of the cockpit.

Trevor did the only thing he could do.

He woke up screaming.

He wasn't in the cockpit anymore, but rather in his sleeping bag underneath a heavy-duty tarp he had set up to keep any rain off him during the night. It took him a moment to gather his bearings, but a metallic clang from outside of his shelter startled him and brought him back to the present.

He grabbed his bow and slowly stepped out of the shelter. The first thing that hit him was the smell—musky and wild. Almost like a wet dog, but not quite. The sun hadn't fully risen yet, but it gave enough sunlight to see his camera tripod had been knocked over and a black bear huffed at him, no more than 25 yards away.

"Hey now," Trevor said.

The bear turned toward him and groaned. It wasn't too big, but it was certainly still big enough to cause some damage if it wanted to. Trevor had seen pictures of black bear attacks, and they were never pretty.

He never took his eyes off the bear as he nocked an arrow. However, the bear huffed one more time and then took off running into the woods before he could even draw the bow. Trevor watched it run off and disappear over the rise.

For some time, he could only watch the hillside, waiting to see if the animal was going to come back around. His heart thundered in his chest, and he couldn't stop his hands from shaking as the adrenaline rush started to disappear.

Finally, convinced it wasn't going to come back anytime soon, he put his bow down and sat on a log next to the firepit. The fire was low, so he put in some more wood. The temperature had dropped significantly during the night, which meant he hadn't gotten much sleep. Trevor had woken up several times to add more wood to the fire.

He grabbed his video recorder and turned it on.

"Well, we had a visitor this morning."

He pointed the camera towards the knocked over tripod and his pot and at some of the bear tracks in the nearby dirt.

"Black bear came in. Probably looking for food and investigating what this new smell was."

Trevor pointed the camera back at himself.

"I'm going to head down to the shore and see if I can get some breakfast and get some more water."

With that, he turned the camera off, grabbed the small GoPro and put it on his head with the provided strap, turned it on, and then gathered his gear to head to the shore. He brought his bow along just in case he came across a rabbit or even a deer. It would also serve if the bear decided to head back this way. However, Trevor had a feeling he might have frightened it off for good when he woke up screaming. A scream like that would have scared him half to death.

The morning air was chilly, but it was a refreshing kind of briskness that he had come to love at a young age. There was something about fresh morning mountain air that got his blood going. Perhaps it was the good memories of his childhood.

Trevor wished his dad were still alive. He knew he'd get a kick watching his son compete on a show like *The Last.* Before the plane crash, they used to watch all those survival shows on television. It was a fun talking point for them both.

One of Trevor's fondest memories of his father was at Thanksgiving about ten years ago when they were all full and tired from a huge feast. Trevor lay on the sofa while his father lounged in the nearby recliner. His mom had just walked in and sat on top of his dad in the recliner. They both laughed and tussled playfully until the show came back on. It was a good day.

His mom died a year later from breast cancer. Her death was the catalyst for a slow decline in the family. She had been the light, and after they laid her to rest, that light had slowly faded.

Trevor wiped a tear away and dug out his fishing line. His plan was to try to catch a fish for breakfast, as it would hopefully give him enough fat and protein to fuel him up for the day, especially since his plan was to get more work done on the shelter.

He found a nice stick he could use to wrap the line around and act as a reel of sorts. Then, he tied the hook on and pulled a grasshopper he had caught yesterday from his pants pocket. It was dead, but Trevor hoped he could convince a fish to go for it.

Trevor found a spot near the shore that looked promising. The water was calm, and it was fairly deep. He tied a small stone onto the line to act as a weight and then flung the line out into the water.

While it didn't land exactly where Trevor wanted, it was close enough that he didn't want to pull the lure back in and try again. After about thirty minutes and nothing to show for his efforts, Trevor cast the line one more time. It landed perfectly.

He decided secure his line and "rod" on shore and get about the business of building his shelter. But first, he needed to check his snares. Trevor had set about six around his camp the day before in hopes of getting a rabbit or squirrel. While the squirrels wouldn't provide much, every little bit counted out in the wild.

He hoped to find a couple of rabbits in his snares. His father used to say hope in one hand and crap in the other and see which one filled up first. Trevor found two things after making the rounds: Jack and shit. They were just as he had left them the day prior.

Before heading back to his camp, Trevor swung back by the water and checked his line. He grabbed the stick and started to reel his line in when something pulled back!

"Holy shit!"

His heart skipped a beat, and he started reeling the line faster. At first it was slack, and he thought perhaps he had snagged it on the bottom as he reeled it in. However, whatever it was jerked the line again and started to pull away from him.

"Oh yeah! Oh yeah! Come to papa!"

Trevor hoped his GoPro would catch this footage, especially when the fish broke water and jumped up into the air. His mind raced with the possibility of a nice meal to keep him energized and the flip side of maybe losing his catch. He'd done enough fishing with standard fishing gear to know that losing a fish was a real threat.

Trevor took his time bringing it closer and closer until finally it was close enough. He yanked the line up, along with the fish, and threw it onto the shore. In an instant, Trevor was on top of it. He grabbed it and moved even further onto shore just in case it slipped out of his hand.

It was a big salmon! One that size would keep him fed for a day or two if he rationed it, and that was exactly what he planned on doing.

"Yes! Thank you!"

He held it out so the GoPro could see it.

"Fuck yes!"

He couldn't believe his luck. Trevor used a nearby rock to kill the fish and then pulled out his knife and got to work gutting and cleaning it. His stomach growled, and he didn't realize just how hungry he was. The last thing he ate was breakfast at the compound yesterday. Trevor was practically salivating as he cleaned the fish.

He picked up his prize and held it up to his face. "You're going to go in my tummy, little buddy!"

Full of happiness, Trevor almost ran back to camp. He was still beaming when his makeshift shelter came into view. However, something made him stop in his tracks.

Pinned to a nearby tree at eye level was a purple envelope with silver filigree. Trevor looked around, but nobody was there.

"Hello?"

Nothing but nature answered.

It was one of the challenge envelopes Randall had spoken about the day before. Trevor placed the fish on a nearby log and opened the challenge.

Use the fish as bait and kill the bear with your bow.

$10,000

"You have to be fucking kidding me. Really?"

A quick search nearby left him even more dumbfounded. There weren't any tracks or traces of whoever had brought the envelope.

"Hello!? Anyone out there?"

Trevor imagined they were nearby filming him to get his full reaction to the envelope. Thoughts raced through his mind as he tried to figure out what to do. How did they get the envelope there without him noticing? He supposed they could have a team of folks who sneaked in and placed them. But the nagging question was how they knew about the fish that he had just caught. Were they watching him via drone? Satellite? Finally, Trevor sat on the log, positioned the camera in front of him, and turned it on.

He showed the envelope to the camera.

"Can you believe this? They want me to use my breakfast as bait to get the bear to come back here and then try to kill it with my bow. Not impossible, but difficult. Not to mention, I have food, right here, right now, that I'll probably waste in this futile attempt."

He could eat the fish and use the calories to guarantee energy. Energy he would need to build the shelter. However, if the plan worked, he would have tons of food with the bear meat, a heavy hide to keep warm, tons of other resources he could scavenge from the bear's body, and an extra $10,000 on top of it regardless of whether or not he finished the show.

With that kind of money, he could pay off his credit card debt and maybe move into a place of his own. It was a gamble.

But he was a gambler.

He stared directly into the camera. “Yeah, let’s do this.”

Instead of working on his shelter, Trevor found an area nearby that looked like a good ambush point. He built a blind out of branches and dead trees. If he was correct, the wind would blow down the hill and towards the sea, perpendicular to where the bear would, hopefully, come in.

Trevor had kept the fish guts, as he planned on using them as extra bait. At the time, he didn’t think he’d be using them, along with the fish, to try and bait a black bear. He planned on setting it all out about twenty yards away from his blind near evening and hoped the bear would come back around to investigate.

If it worked, he’d be set up nicely for quite some time. If it didn’t, he may have just hurt his chances of winning. Trevor hoped luck was in his favor.

Chapter Ten

Lucy groaned as her stomach growled. A moment later, cramps rolled through her body causing her to have to sit down. She was lightheaded and fatigued, all signs that she wasn't getting enough food.

This morning marked the seventh day since they had dropped her off. Overall, things were going well. Lucy had caught two rabbits in her snares but had devoured them quicker than she anticipated. She had even caught a fish two days ago. But soon after the meals were gone, there was a lingering hunger that concerned her.

Lucy wasn't a stranger to starvation. Growing up with her family came with certain privileges, one of those privileges being eating on a daily basis. Her father had taken away food for five days once because he caught her looking at dresses in her mom's Sears catalog. The beating hurt, but the starvation was worse.

This was different. Stronger somehow. Plus, the lack of sleep, cold seeping into her bones, and general fatigue were all taking their toll. This was the true nature of survival—trying to scrape enough food, water, and warmth to keep alive, while battling against a constant enemy force trying to sap your resources. Only, instead of this being a castle under siege, she was the castle, and the enemy was the environment.

Perhaps it was everything else playing into it as well—her mind playing tricks on her, trying to get her to tap out. The thought of a nice steak and lobster dinner made her mouth water and her stomach complain again.

It was time to get her mind focused on other things. She stretched and turned on the camera.

"Well, it's another beautiful morning here!"

She turned the camera from her face and panned all around, taking care to get some great shots of the sunrise and the serene trees. It wasn't a lie; it was one of the most beautiful places she'd seen in a long time. However, there was a ravenous hunger that afflicted *everything* around her. The rabbits she had caught were tiny, barely more than skin and bones. The squirrels she had seen in the trees were just as thin. Everything she came across felt like it wanted to devour her down to the marrow.

"It's time for breakfast, and I don't have anything to eat, so let's go see what we can find."

Lucy turned the big camera off and powered on the GoPro. It gave a loud beep indicating it was on and ready to capture whatever she came across.

She took another step just as a wave of dizziness hit.

"Whoa there..."

She sat down again and waited for it to pass. It was concerning for sure, but she hoped getting some nutrients in her, and some fresh water might help.

She retrieved her pot and secured it to her bag. To help with her balance, Lucy grabbed a long branch and whittled it smooth. It would make for a great walking stick.

"Okay, second try."

This time when she stood, the light-headedness hit her again, but not as bad. After a couple of shaky steps, she was on her way.

Lucy had made the rounds so many times in the past week, she thought she could probably navigate her trap lines in the dark without incident. It was as if she were on autopilot. Lucy scanned the ground as she walked by each snare, looking for fur or movement.

They were all empty.

"Damn it!"

As much as she didn't want to expend the energy—energy she greatly needed to finish her shelter—Lucy knew she needed food. It was time to expand her walkabout and forage for mushrooms and berries.

Lucy had already harvested all the edible plants and fungus around her camp. Her plan was to walk out further this time, maybe a quarter mile at most, and make a big circle. Hopefully, she would come across more of the tasty chanterelle mushrooms.

At least the sun was out, and it was a nice day. Not too hot, not cold. As she walked, a nearby raven cawed and another not too far away answered. It hadn't been more than ten minutes when she found her first patch of Oregon grapes!

"Yes!"

She hustled over and pointed the GoPro towards them.

"These little guys are great. A little sour, but they might help my stomach cramps, actually."

Lucy collected a bunch and stored them in the large pocket of her jacket. She grabbed her walking stick and stood up. Knowing that she had something to eat made her feel a little better.

She continued her journey, finding a few more grapes. However, local critters had eaten all the mushrooms she came across already. Lucy harvested what she could, but it was a meager haul.

It had been a few hours since she left, and Lucy started to worry she was burning more energy than it was worth at this point. Besides, she wanted to get back to camp and prepare what she had found.

Just before she turned to head back, the wind shifted, bringing the pungent stink of rotting meat to her nose. Lucy put an arm across her face and looked around. She couldn't see the animal; however, more ravens cawed in the distance.

"Better go check it out. It may be fresh enough to save some of the meat… whatever it is. I'll go in slow just in case there are still predators around," she said, more for the GoPro than anything else.

It wasn't hard to find. The smell got worse the closer she walked, plus more ravens had shown up. Some even made circles in the air about two hundred yards away.

"Bingo."

Whatever it was, it was up a small hill leading towards the rocky mountains nearby. Her walking stick made the going a little easier, but it was still work to get up. Lucy took care with her footing, as she didn't want to fall and break an ankle or twist her knee. An injury like that would send her home.

The cacophony of caws became louder until she pushed through the brush and scared the unkindness away. They screamed at her as they flew to the nearby trees, annoyed at her intrusion.

The first thing that caught her eye was a rack of antlers followed by the grayish brown hide. A dead buck deer lay on its side near a large boulder. Blood stained the rocks, and flies buzzed about the animal's corpse in a chaotic frenzy.

This close, the stench was almost unbearable. Lucy walked around to get away from the wind. It made it a little better, but it was still bad enough that she could almost taste it through her open mouth.

From this angle, Lucy found a long cut along the deer's flank. Whatever had injured it had also opened the guts, as the stomach and some of the intestines had pushed through the wound.

Its hide was a mess, and some of the antlers were broken. Lucy looked at the rocky hillside and saw a trail of blood and gore leading up.

"It looks like something attacked this animal and it ran away, only to die here. From the looks of it, it's been dead maybe a couple of days. It's hard to say though, without—"

Something caught her eye. At first, she thought it was dried blood, but the color was slightly off. Lucy covered her face again and crept closer. Near the wound was more of that mossy red substance she had found on the dead moose. However, this time, it was vibrant in color. Flesh-colored 'berries' dotted the moss as well.

Lucy used the end of her walking stick to try to move the deer a bit and get a better look at the underside of the wound, but when she touched it, the deer shuddered and hissed.

She scrambled back until she slammed into a rock. Pain flared up her backside.

"Ow, fuck!"

Lucy didn't dare take her eyes off the deer. Visions of it getting up on shaky legs and stumbling in her direction filled her mind. She was sure that at any moment it would turn its head toward her with a sick crack and stare at her with milky white eyes like it had just jumped out of a cheesy horror movie from the 80s.

Yet, it did none of those things.

Her heart fluttered. Lucy chuckled and rubbed her sore back. It hurt to touch, but she thought it was maybe just a bruise. Hopefully, nothing more than that.

"I thought it was still alive somehow. I guess it was just gasses escaping or something. I think I'll just leave this deer alone. Besides, whatever wounded it might be around."

As if on cue, some rocks shifted nearby and clattered down a game trail. Lucy froze and snapped her head in the sound's direction. For what felt like forever, Lucy held her breath and watched. However, nothing moved again, but she couldn't shake the feeling that something was watching her.

Finally, Lucy exhaled and stood. She made herself as big as could be, hopefully intimidating whatever was up there, and slowly back stepped out of the area.

"It's okay, you can have it," she said.

Lucy made it to the brush where she had first seen the deer and turned to leave.

"Lucy?"

She froze.

It was her dead brother's voice.

Chapter Eleven

Trevor sat in the makeshift blind he'd built out of various logs, sticks, and tree branches. He'd lost track of time, but the sun was beginning to set. It made for a picturesque scene with a brilliant display of autumnal colors, but it was the last thing on his mind.

He was hungry.

It was a deep hunger he wasn't used to that dominated every thought in his brain. It had been a few days since he caught the fish, and now it sat rotting, stuck to a tree branch at chest level. He hoped putting it a little higher might help the scent to travel further.

What a waste it had been. He'd contemplated eating some of it and using the rest, but Trevor wasn't sure if that would disqualify him from winning the ten grand if the bear happened to return and he somehow landed a great shot with his bow. In the end, he decided to try and bait the bear.

As he sat behind his blind and stared at the fish, now home to flies, his mind wandered to dark places. There was a small part of him that thought about eating it anyway, even though it would make him sick. But there was something deep in his psyche that reveled in the thought of tearing the putrid meat from the bones and slurping them down.

He had caught another fish earlier that morning, and the moment he put some of the cooked meat past his lips was pure bliss. His mouth had watered at the thought of ripping into its scaly flesh, but for some reason, it did little to sate the pit in his stomach. In fact, after he finished, he almost felt hungrier than before he ate.

He closed his eyes and took a deep breath to clear his head.

With the sun disappearing behind the mountains, the chill crept in. It was time to call it a night and try again tomorrow. Ultimately, Trevor decided to keep the bait out, but he would need some sort of warning system to wake him if the bear decided to come by.

Trevor had found some old, rusted tin cans while searching his area the day before. He used some cordage to tie them together and lash them to the branch with the fish. If anything moved the branch, the cans would rattle, and he'd hear it from camp.

Satisfied with the setup, Trevor gathered his bow and wandered back to his shelter. The fire smoldered, but it wasn't difficult to feed it and get a good blaze going again.

The warmth of the flames was nice. It wasn't even the cold season yet, but when the sun went down, it got cold. He glanced over and cringed when he saw just how little progress he'd made on his long-term shelter. Trevor vowed that if the bear didn't come around by tomorrow morning, he'd abandon the challenge and get back to work on the important things.

If he didn't have it done before the snow came...

The cans rattled!

Trevor snapped his head toward the sound and listened. At first, there was nothing, and he thought maybe it was a false alarm. But then it rattled again. And then again, followed by a soft huff and groan.

The bear was back!

Trevor grabbed his bow, turned on the GoPro, and made his way toward the blind, ensuring the wind wasn't going to blow his scent right through to the bear. He took care with each step, going as fast as he dared while still moving quietly. It was dark out, but the full moon provided enough light to navigate.

It wasn't long before the blind came into view. He couldn't quite make out anything past it though. Luckily, the wind was in his face, and the odor of rotting fish hit his nose.

Another huff and groan came from in front of him, not far from the blind. The cans rattled again, and he jumped a little at the noise. Trevor's heart pounded as he closed the distance. He did his best to try to control his breathing, but the excitement of the situation was getting the better of him. Not only was there $10K at stake, but a really good meal as well.

He nocked an arrow and crept into his blind. He expected to see the bear's shape in the darkness; however, what he saw made his heart drop into the pit of his stomach.

The fish was gone, and the bear was nowhere to be seen. He was too late.

"Damn it!" he whispered under his breath. Trevor looked all around, but there was nothing but a few broken limbs and a bit of fish guts on the ground.

To get a better view, he turned his headlamp on, but he made sure it was on the low, red light setting. He stood, exposing himself to the bear if it was still out there, but it gave him a better view.

He looked at the trees, hoping to find the animal, but it must have heard him coming, or maybe the wind had shifted and given him away. His mind started playing a game of what if, telling him he should have stayed in the blind and waited. Or what if he had just run when he first heard the noise?

Trevor's body deflated with dejection, and he turned to head back to his camp. He had only taken two steps when the cans rattled again.

He whipped around, and his light caught the eyes of something just at the tree line.

It was the bear!

It stared at him with a line of drool dripping from its muzzle. The bear huffed at him and moved closer, sniffing the branch where the fish had been, then licking up some of the remaining guts on the ground.

Trevor brought his bow up and took aim. The bear faced towards him with its head down. It wasn't a good angle for a shot. As he waited for the bear to turn, he couldn't help but notice just how thin it was. At this time of the year, bears should be getting ready for hibernation and growing as fat as possible, but this bear was nothing more than skin and bone. In fact, he wasn't even sure if it was the same bear that had shown up at his camp earlier.

He wondered if it would matter whether or not he killed this one or if it had to be the other one to meet the $10K challenge. Regardless, Trevor decided he would harvest this bear if it would only give him a good angle.

As if it had heard his thoughts, the bear looked right at Trevor and stood on its hind legs, offering him a clear view of its vitals. Trevor raised his bow and drew back.

A loud snap that was more akin to a small tree breaking rather than a branch sounded off to the right. The bear dropped to all fours and turned towards the noise. Trevor let up on the draw and turned as well, trying to see what had just happened.

Had a tree fallen? Was it another bear?

The wind shifted and with it brought a rotting stench that made Trevor gag. The bear growled once and then turned tail, bounding off through the trees.

"Fuck!"

Whatever had made the noise gave chase, barreling through more trees and branches, causing a racket that sounded like a bulldozer crashing through the forest. Trevor stood still, unsure of what to do.

The crashing got louder, and for half a second, the shadowy shape of something large flashed behind the trees and branches ahead of him.

The bear growled again, further away now. Much further away. It always amazed Trevor just how fast they could run if they wanted to.

More cracks and snaps, and then there came a noise that Trevor had never heard before in his life. It was a strange howl that was a mix between an elk bugle, mountain lion growl, coyote yip, and most disturbing, a human scream.

It made Trevor's legs begin to shake and his blood run cold.

In the distance, the bear growled and roared but was cut off mid-cry. Then came a wet rip followed by the bear's death groan, a long, drawn-out moan of pain and anger.

Trevor stood for a few moments before finally sneaking back to his camp. He didn't know what was out there, but he didn't want it coming back for him. After returning, he fed the fire, building it higher and hotter than he would have preferred, but he hoped it would keep whatever was out there away from his camp.

He didn't sleep at all that night. Instead, he kept his eyes on the woods and his hand on his bow.

Chapter Twelve

Randall was busy flipping through a newspaper from 1913 when one of the techs, a Ms. Abigail Marks from Minnesota, cleared her throat next to him. Of course, he'd felt her walk up; the nervous energy and uncertainty had its own unique flavor.

Randall continued to read the paper, not even turning his head to acknowledge her. Abigail was about to say something when Randall held a hand up to stop her.

"What can I do for you, Ms. Marks?"

"Uh..." Abigail swallowed hard. "Um..."

"If you came over here to stutter and stammer, you can turn right around and leave. I'm not in the mood."

The comment made her even more anxious. Randall kept a smile from reaching his face, but he did find it entertaining to mess with the help from time to time.

"He has awoken and left His den," Abigail said.

Again, something he had felt earlier. But why let the poor girl know that? Randall put the newspaper down and looked her straight in the eye. His gaze bore through her like a drill. "And where is He now?"

Abigail closed her eyes. "I don't know."

"I suggest you find Him, then, Ms. Marks."

Something about the cool tone of his voice made her even more afraid than if he had screamed at her.

"Of course, right away!"

She scrambled back to her desk, almost tripping on the way back.

Randall watched her go and wondered if all humans were this incompetent or just the ones that happened to always surround him. Still, he couldn't suppress a smile.

He'd labored for centuries, making deals with things that had no name, gathering information, searching the dark ends of the globe looking for any signs of He Who Shall Devour the Stars. This time, his work would come to fruition, and he will have carved himself a place amongst the shadowy and eldritch. This time, he would get what he deserved.

Randall sat back down and picked up a red phone on his desk. There wasn't a need to dial any number, as it automatically called another phone it was slaved to. After two rings, someone picked up.

"It's begun," Randall said.

"Excellent," replied Ms. Thomas.

Randall hung and took a drink of coffee, savoring its bold flavor, and returned to reading the newspaper.

Lucy grabbed her walking stick and her bag of supplies. The morning sun had just begun to peek above the horizon, and she was eager to go check her snares. It had been a few days since she last ate anything, and she was *hungry*.

By all accounts, she shouldn't feel this way, not yet. However, here she was, wondering if that red moss was edible—most likely not—or what boot leather tasted like.

Before she left, Lucy propped the camera up and turned it on. She sat next to the fire and poked at the coals with a stick, unsure of what to say.

"I'm hungry."

She looked directly into the camera now.

"It's bad. I'm starting to wonder if I have some sort of parasite inside me. Everything I eat does so little to help. It's like a need, a primal desire that has set deep into my bones... unlike anything I've ever experienced before. I've been starving a few times in my life, but it never felt like this. This is something else."

Lucy used the stick to roll a small log closer to the flames. She watched it smoke and eventually catch.

"It's been almost two weeks, which means the medical teams will be out here soon to evaluate me. I don't want to tell them about my hunger levels, but I feel like I can't hide it either."

Lucy pulled her shirt up, exposing her abdomen. Her ribs were visibly pronounced.

"I was never very big, but this is not good. It's only been two weeks! It's not like I haven't eaten anything! I mean, come on."

Tears welled in her eyes. The whole thing was frustrating, and the HRT seemed to ramp up her emotions ever since she had started her transition. She wiped the tears away with her sleeve before using the walking stick to help her stand. A wave of dizziness hit, and Lucy almost had to sit back down.

"All I can hope is that I have trapped a rabbit or two and I can have something to eat. I've already devoured all the berries and mushrooms around my camp. If I don't find something to eat soon..."

Lucy couldn't finish the sentence. With that, Lucy turned the camera off, turned her GoPro on, and began her circular trek around the area to check her snares.

As she came to the first snare, her heart jumped. A patch of gray fur stuck out just below the low-lying branch where she had secured the wire.

Lucy let out a cry of excitement and rushed over to the snare, but that cry died in her throat.

She had caught a rabbit for sure, but something else had come along and tore it to pieces. Fur, blood, and bone decorated the site. Most of the rabbit itself was gone, except a part of its head, half a torso, and its foot that was still caught in the snare.

"Jesus fucking Christ!"

Lucy crouched down next to the rabbit. Some of it might be salvageable, though it wouldn't be much. But calories were calories, and there was still a little hide left she could use to make cordage.

Lucy used the end of her walking stick to move the rabbit. It was stuck to the ground. At first, Lucy thought maybe it had frozen there overnight. However, as she pushed with the stick, the rabbit's body twitched.

She let out a scream and backed away. No way was it still alive. It was in literal pieces. It had to be something else. Lucy pushed the viscera with the stick again. It squirmed under her touch. Maybe maggots or something had already gotten to work on it. She moved it one more time, using the end of the stick to push it up, and found the culprit.

An acrid odor reached her nose when it came free and revealed that same red moss as before. Bits of the moss stretched with the body like some sort of sticky glue. When Lucy finally flipped the carcass over, the moss had either burrowed into the body or burst out of the body, she couldn't quite tell which.

Fleshy berries had sprouted all over the moss and on the animal's carcass where it touched. Each berry was about the size of a dime, spherical, and a pale, skin-tone color. As she stared in horror, something pulsed in the berries.

Lucy crouched down, using her walking stick to steady herself to get a closer look. The berries had something inside them. They were somewhat transparent and slender, and wormlike shapes swam around inside the berries. It reminded her of an egg sack or something similar, and as soon as she imagined it, she wished she hadn't. Visions of tiny spiders bursting out of each berry and scrambling towards made her hair stand on end.

Lucy didn't want anything to do with it anymore. She stood, flipped the rabbit back to where it had originally lay, and moved on to the next site. Whatever that moss or fungus was, it couldn't be good. It was better to just leave it alone.

She meandered her trail for a minute before coming to the next spot. There was another rabbit caught in her snare!

She rushed over to it but stopped as soon as the red moss came into view. Just like the last spot, this one had a half-eaten rabbit. This one was worse off. The red moss almost completely covered the dead animal. At first, she thought it was still alive, as rabbit looked like it was breathing. Yet, when she looked closer, it was the moss itself that pulsated.

Lucy's stomach growled at her, and cramps wracked her body. She fought through the discomfort and continued her trek. One after another, she found the same grisly scene. It was strange enough that each of her snares had caught a rabbit, but stranger still that they all suffered from whatever the moss was.

It was a mental blow that hit her harder than the hunger itself. Lucy fought back tears of frustration and decided to get to work. Whatever predator lurking around had compromised the snares, plus the moss. She found a few more sites, closer to her camp this time, with the hopes that she would maybe hear the animal struggling and could get to it before whatever else was out there.

Lucy was busy setting a snare next to an old pine that was broken in half and burned out from a lightning strike. It was on the path that some squirrels liked to use, so it was a decent spot. As she worked on the snare wire, something caught her eye, the glint of something shiny near the gnarled root of the tree.

Lucy crawled over and wiped some of the dirt and debris away, exposing a small container. It was just like the battery container the staff had issued her—black, semi-transparent plastic, and waterproof. There was something inside.

She grabbed the container and pulled it free. Inside were some batteries that would fit her camera equipment as well as a single memory card. It was the same kind she used to film herself at camp.

This had to have belonged to a previous contestant. Maybe it dropped out of their pack at some point. It was strange though, as the spot she was in was somewhat out of the way. With a shrug, she put the container in her pack and headed back. She'd give it to the medical team when they arrived.

By the time she got to camp, she was fatigued and ready to call it a night. However, she was also cold. Lucy stoked the fire and got it burning hot. For what felt like hours, she stared at the flames until finally she was warm once again.

The hunger was intense, and she tried every trick she could think of to take her mind off it. The desire to rend the flesh off one of those rabbits drilled deep into her mind and wouldn't let up.

Then, it hit her. The medical team had never arrived at her location. It was odd, as they were very specific about which day they would show up. Hopefully, she hadn't missed them while she was out checking snares. She was sure they would have yelled her name or came looking, wouldn't they? Perhaps they had to take one of the other contestants off the island. If that were the case, her odds of winning had just increased.

It was late, and since there was no food to be had, Lucy decided to get some sleep. Maybe a good night's rest would help reset things. Tomorrow, she would try and catch some fish if her snares didn't pan out again.

She threw another log into the fire and headed into her shelter. Before she could shed her boots, something on the bed caught her eye.

An envelope sat on her sleeping bag.

"What the...?"

Lucy shimmied over to it and picked it up. Underneath the envelope was a large, jagged rock stained with what looked like blood.

Her breathing became labored as she opened the envelope and read the letter inside.

Kill the rabbit with the rock. $5,000.

"What? What rabbit? They were all already dea—"

Before she could finish, the childlike screams of a scared rabbit filled the night air.

Chapter Thirteen

The rabbit's scream pierced Lucy's ears, causing her to cringe and drop the rock. A chill ran up her spine, and the small hairs on her arms and neck stood straight.

"No... no, this isn't real. It can't be real."

Lucy fumbled with her video recorder. She needed to get this on tape, if only to be able to prove to herself and others that what was happening wasn't some figment of her imagination like her dead brother's voice coming from the darkness.

It took her several attempts, fingers fumbling over the equipment. All the while, the rabbit continued to cry in fear, but Lucy finally got the camera turned on. She pointed it outside the door of her shelter and held her breath.

"So... uh..." She couldn't form the words. They stuck in her throat and held on for dear life. Lucy grabbed the pot of water and brought it up to her mouth. A lot of it spilled down her chin and onto her chest, soaking her clothes, but some of the cool liquid finally made it in. It felt good going down and helped her regain focus.

"So... I was about to go to bed when I saw this. Lucy turned the light on the camera and then pointed to her sleeping bag where the envelope and rock sat. She fumbled with the envelope with one hand

and opened it up for the camera. "It says I need to kill the rabbit with this rock, and I get $5K."

Lucy dropped the envelope and picked up the rock. "Why is it already bloody? And why…?" Lucy shook her head. No, she was rambling. "It doesn't matter. Apparently, I need to go kill this rabbit."

Lucy grabbed the rock with one hand and held the camera with the other. She shuffled out of her shelter and into the night. As soon as the cold air hit her wet shirt, it began to chill her core. But that sensation wasn't at the forefront of her mind. The rabbit, the rock, and what she had to do dominated her thoughts.

The landscape felt different in the darkness. She'd probably walked this area dozens upon dozens of times already and knew it like the back of her hand at this point. However, something was off this time. The trees were closer now, giving her a strange and uncomfortable feeling of claustrophobia.

The light that came off the camera was bright, but it cast odd shadows as she moved, shadows that danced and swirled as she walked closer to the screaming rabbit. Lucy did her best to ignore it and keep moving forward.

The cry was getting louder, and from the sound of it, the rabbit had gotten caught on the snare furthest from camp. Lucy cursed under her breath and picked up her pace. By the time she was about ten yards away, the screams were almost deafening.

"I'm coming!"

The rabbit must have seen the light coming because its cries picked up in intensity. She couldn't quite see it yet but knew the snare would come into view in mere moments. Suddenly, something made her stop.

The rabbit's cries changed in pitch and tone until they sounded just like a human child crying.

It sounded too much like her younger brother when he was a kid. It was too human.

The poor animal continued to wail. She wanted nothing more than for it to stop, for all of this to go away as if it were a bad dream. But she had a duty, and the longer she waited, the longer the poor creature had to suffer. Lucy took a wary step forward, and the light from the camera went out. When it did, the rabbit's cries fell silent.

"Fuck."

Lucy tried to find the button that would turn the light back on, but no matter how many times she tried or how hard she smashed it, the light didn't return. The darkness smothered her, wrapping itself around her body like a wet blanket. Her heart threatened to burst out of her chest, and it took all her willpower not to turn tail and run back to her shelter. She had left the satphone back at camp. It was stupid, as she had been instructed to keep it on her person at all times in case she got injured, but in the moment, she'd forgotten to grab it.

Lucy fought the urge to run back to camp and call the number in the speed dial and have them come pick her up as soon as possible. But that was fear talking. And while fear had a convincing argument, it was one she had heard many times before. But then the conversation took a different turn.

Something big moved through the trees in the distance, back towards the mountains and the center of the island. Branches snapped as they moved. From the sound of it, it was quite large, probably a bear coming to eat the little rabbit.

An idea popped into her head. The camera had a night vision setting.

Lucy cradled the rock in her armpit while she navigated through the camera's menu. Finally, she found it. With a push of a button, the camera switched modes.

Through the tiny monitor, the forest came to life as the lens picked up any available light out there. It wasn't ideal, but at least she could see again.

Whatever moved through the trees was still a ways away from her, but it was getting closer. Probably a bear in search of a quick meal.

If she wanted to get the money and win the challenge, she would have to act fast. Her instincts yelled at her to just run back to camp and build the fire up as high as she could possibly make it, but there was a small part of her brain that wanted the money. She hadn't had $5K in her account all at once for... well, ever. And there was an even bigger part of her brain that wanted the food. Lucy's stomach rumbled in agreement.

"Okay, really quick, get in there, kill the rabbit with the rock, get out. If we can get the rabbit free before the bear gets much closer, bonus."

Lucy spoke for the camera, but really it was more for herself. She imagined that exact scenario of rushing in and finishing the rabbit off with a quick blow. In reality, she crept forward, trying to be as quiet as possible.

She crested the small rise, and the rabbit came into view. Through the camera, all she could see was its little body pulling against the snare as hard as it could. The rabbit started to scream again, fighting harder against the snare.

"It's okay."

It was most certainly not okay.

As Lucy talked, the rabbit flipped around and faced her. Dark liquid covered the front of its mouth and fur. It was hard to tell with the night vision, but it looked like blood. The thing was gaunt as well—even through its fur she could see the raised impression of small ribs, kind of like how her ribs looked.

One of its eyes glowed on screen; the other was just a gory pit where the eye should have been. The front leg caught in the snare dangled at an odd angle and was also covered in blood. Lucy zoomed in with the camera to get a better look.

"No way..."

It was blood on its fur but mixed with that blood was more of the moss. The little berries gave it away. Despite the chaos of the situation, disappointment settled into her marrow. She wouldn't be eating this rabbit either.

"I'm so sorry little guy. It will be over soon," Lucy said in her most soothing voice.

She switched the camera and the rock, putting the rock in her dominant hand. She'd be able to swing harder and have better aims.

Another branch snapped. Closer this time. It was hard to judge, especially with the rabbit scared out of its mind so close, but Lucy figured it was probably within 500 yards. She had to act fast.

"Okay, I'll make this as quick as possible."

Lucy clutched the rock and inched closer. The rabbit took one look at her, and instead of shying away, it lunged right at her face.

Lucy let out a yell as the rabbit's teeth snapped together less than an inch away from her nose. She fell on her butt and scrambled backward.

"What the fuck?!"

Without the aid of the camera, she couldn't see clearly, but the rabbit's dark shape bounced around in a struggle to get free. Lucy grabbed the camera and pointed it back towards the rabbit.

The animal frothed at the mouth, its remaining eye bulging in what she was all too familiar with—rage. Lucy had heard of trapped or cornered animals getting violent to save themselves, but this was something else. The rabbit pulled against the snare with all its strength as it tried to get closer to her.

It wanted to *hurt* her. Lucy could almost taste the desire in the air as it rolled off the rabbit. She could feel its urge to sink its teeth into her flesh and tear it away so it could crack into a bone and get all her juicy marrow.

She knew she should run and let whatever was coming finish the rabbit off. It was clearly diseased. Could rabbits get rabies?

Yet the money sang its siren song. The rabbit was just an arm's length away. As long as it didn't dart away, she figured she could brain it with the rock easily enough.

The rabbit pulled against the snare with all its strength, skin and muscle tearing. It would get out soon, perhaps without a leg, but the way it was coming at her, Lucy knew it would still try and attack even with such a grievous injury.

Lucy took a deep breath in to try and calm her nerves. Then, she let it out and struck. The rock crushed the rabbit's skull with a sickening crunch.

It fell to the ground on its side, twitching. It stared at her with its good eye and then tried to get up.

"Come on!"

Lucy brought the rock down again.

The rabbit started its childlike wail once more. Lucy smashed it again, harder and harder until her hand was numb. The rabbit cried louder with each strike. Lucy's ears rang, and she could taste blood in her mouth.

"Die! Why won't you die?!"

The thing in the woods crashed closer to her. Lucy registered the sound in the back of her mind, but she didn't care anymore. She had to kill this rabbit.

The rabbit's wails finally cut off, and the forest fell silent. It was as if the entire world held its breath, waiting and watching.

Tears ran down Lucy's cheeks and into the dirt. She had long ago dropped the camera so she could use both hands to bring the rock down on the rabbit. The poor animal was nothing more than blood, brain, and fur.

And red moss.

Lucy let the rock fall out of her hand, and she slid away from the rabbit as far as her arms and legs would take her before she broke down.

Heavy, chest-wracking sobs rattled her body as she curled up on the ground in the fetal position and cried.

"I'm sorry... I am so, so, sorry..."

Lucy rolled onto her back and looked up into the night sky. The trees, seeming to tower above her like giant skeletal fingers, considered her with indifference.

She wiped her eyes with her coat sleeve. Gore covered her hands, still shaky from what had just happened. She hoped it was just blood and fur, but she knew some of that moss had probably gotten on her as well. Lucy needed to wash her hands as quickly as possible.

Her throat was raw from screaming and crying, and her entire body shook as the adrenaline wore off and the reality of what had just happened hit her.

Perhaps it was time to tap out.

Lucy propped herself up on one elbow and started to rise when one of the trees moved above her. She froze. The tree twisted and turned, almost looking at her. That's when she realized it wasn't a tree at all.

It was antlers. Similar to those of a large bull elk, but twisting and chaotic.

The thing moved again and lumbered off back towards the mountains. Whatever it was, it was big. Bigger than anything Lucy had ever seen.

Chapter Fourteen

Trevor stood on the bank and cast his line out into the water. The surface barely moved, with only a gentle lapping at the shore. The sun had come up just an hour ago, and he was thankful. With each passing day, it got colder and colder. This morning, he woke up and could barely feel his hands and feet. The sun's warmth was a welcome respite. Besides, the way the sunlight sparkled off the water was magical. The whole scene would have been magical too, if he weren't so damn hungry.

He couldn't stop thinking about the bear. A big part of him wanted to go see if he could find the body, because it was for sure dead. He'd heard bears give off that death groan before. But something in his gut told him to stay away from it.

Another thing that bothered him was the fact that the medical crew never showed up yesterday. During orientation, they had been adamant about their schedules. Perhaps they had their hands full with another person.

Trevor's stomach cramped, causing him to double over. The cramps were getting worse as time went by. It was why he was down at the shore trying to catch a fish instead of working on his shelter.

He was about to give up when his line went taut. Fighting through the cramps, Trevor pulled back and could feel the fish struggling to get away on the other end.

"Oh yeah, come to papa!"

He reeled it in and somehow got it up on the bank without it jumping free from the hook. Dropping the stick that served as a reel, he grabbed the fish with both hands to secure it. Then, with a quick blow from a nearby rock, he ended its life quickly.

This one was going to go into his belly, no matter what new challenge showed up. Trevor cleaned the fish up and headed back to camp. He kept expecting to see another envelope with another crazy challenge in it, but there was none when he got back.

Trevor skewered the fish lengthwise with a stick he had already used for cooking then placed it over the fire, using rocks on either end to hold the fish up above coals. His mouth salivated as the aroma of cooked meat hit his nostrils, and it took every bit of his willpower not to devour the fish right then and there.

After a few more moments, it was ready. Trevor grabbed the skewer and pulled it away from the fire. He pulled some of the meat and it slid off the small, translucent bones with ease. Without a second thought, he shoved it into his mouth.

It was pure ecstasy. Trevor sighed with relief, even though it was still very hot. He wished he had some seasoning or lemon to accompany it, but beggars couldn't be choosers, and he consumed the fish in record time.

As he took the last bite, he immediately wanted more. The emptiness in his stomach wasn't satisfied in the least, and somehow, he was hungrier than before. He still had the fish head and had planned on making a stew later; however, the thought of sticking the head in his mouth and crunching through the bone to get to the brain was a titillating concept.

Something moved through the trees not too far away. Trevor looked up from the fish remains and eyed the trees. It was probably the medical crew finally coming to check on him. As much as he was worried they would find something wrong and send him home, he looked forward to the human interaction. For the past couple of weeks, he'd only had himself and the camera to talk to.

"I'm over here!" Trevor yelled.

He scooped the fish remains up and placed them in his cooking pot, then he hung the pot up on a high branch for later. Perhaps he could find some mushrooms or something to put in the stew alongside the fish head.

Trevor did a quick cleanup of his site—not that there was much to clean—but he wanted to ensure he presented himself and his living conditions in the best possible light. He berated himself for not getting more done on his permanent shelter, but there wasn't anything he could do about it now.

The sound of something brushing by the trees, like a person's coat or something, sounded not too far away. Trevor tried to see if he could detect movement, but he didn't spy anything.

"Hello! Over here!"

Nothing.

Trevor waited a few more minutes and then thought maybe it was an animal. An animal meant possible food. He grabbed his bow and turned on his GoPro camera before sneaking toward the direction of the sound.

Although Trevor tried to stay focused on hunting and staying quiet, his mind wandered. He couldn't help it. Why hadn't the team showed up yet? What was in the trees moving around? The whole thing didn't sit well with him. That and the fact that he was hungry just made it all a big ball of shit in his brain.

After about two dozen steps, Trevor stopped and listened. He hoped he would hear the crew talking as they made their way up from the shore towards his camp, but the forest was silent. It wasn't just void of humans speaking. No birds chirped. No squirrels chattered. Hell, even the bugs had gone quiet.

He nocked an arrow in his bow just in case it was another bear or maybe a wolf. Trevor followed a well-used game trail, keeping the wind at his face the best he could. His steps were measured as he took care where he placed each foot. He almost considered shedding his boots to reduce the noise of his stalk but ultimately decided against it. There were too many sharp rocks and wet puddles.

A twig snapped nearby.

Trevor stopped and held his breath as he listened. At first, there was nothing, but soon there was a strange, swishing noise.

It was rhythmic, almost like breathing but faster. And it was getting closer.

Another branch snapped, and Trevor realized too late that the swish was the sound a coat made when someone was running.

Running right at him.

Trevor turned just as a human figure burst through the brush and hit him at full speed. The air was blasted from his lungs when they landed. The attacker rained down a flurry of blows aimed at Trevor's face. The first couple connected and started his ears ringing, but out of instinct, Trevor brought his arms up to protect himself.

He wanted to yell *stop*, but he couldn't form the words, as he hadn't regained his breath yet. Whoever was on top of him wasn't as heavy as he expected, so Trevor bucked his hips and pushed to the side. His attacker hit the ground, and he rolled over on top.

Charlize struggled under his weight and tried to claw at his throat. He gripped her wrists and pinned them down onto the ground.

"Stop!"

His voice was ragged, but at least he could breathe again. If Charlize registered what he had just yelled, it didn't show. She screamed and growled, trying her best to break free. Trevor wasn't ready for how strong she was, and she twisted out of his grip. Her hands flew towards his neck, and he scrambled back to avoid the attack.

Charlize sat up and got to her feet but remained crouched low like some sort of wild animal. Trevor got to his feet as well and held his hands out in front of his body.

"Charlize! It's me, Trevor."

The look in her eyes was feral and hungry. She began to circle around him, but he circled as well.

Her jacket was torn in several places and stained with blood, and there were what appeared to be claw marks ripped into her pants. Blood oozed from the wounds, running down her legs and into her boots.

"It's okay, calm down. I'm not going to hurt you unless you force me," Trevor said.

Charlize lunged forward and took a swipe at him. He ducked under the blow and came up fast, grabbing her body. Before she could swipe again, he spun her around so her back was to him and put her in a bear hug.

She fought to try and get free, but he had leverage now, which he used to take her to the ground. Trevor pinned her under his body.

Charlize wailed and screamed, and again, her strength was immense. It took everything he had to keep her pinned.

"Calm down, please! Charlize!"

Finally, she stopped struggling and began sobbing. Unsure of what to do, Trevor held her pinned for a few more moments before warily releasing some of the pressure. He sighed in relief when she didn't immediately try to attack him again.

Trevor let her go and sat against a nearby tree. He was covered in sweat, and his lungs burned with the exertion of what had just happened.

Charlize lay on the ground crying, eventually hugging her knees.

"What the fuck happened? Why are you covered in the blood, and why did you try and kill me?"

At first, she didn't answer, but then she spoke, barely more than a whisper. Trevor had to get closer to hear her.

"What?" he asked.

Charlize turned and looked at him. Her eyes had lost that wild look, replaced now with absolute fear.

She pointed back to the trees. "Something is out there."

Chapter Fifteen

Lucy finished applying the pine sap glue around the rabbit sinew lashings on her spear. She had been up most of the night knapping a piece of flint she had found earlier into a broad, leaf-shaped, Clovis spearpoint. It had taken longer than it should have due to her exhaustion, hunger, and her mind being in other places. Lucy couldn't stop thinking about that *thing* in the woods—how tall it was and the deep fear that permeated her spine when it had moved next to her.

There was something about it that made her insides crawl. It wasn't normal; she knew that without having to study the creature. There was nothing she'd come across in this world that instilled that kind of fear in her before, that feeling of *insignificance*. That was the word that bounced into her mind later. When it had moved and the realization of it hit her, there was a moment when she had felt like the tiniest thing in the world. That *thing* didn't care about her, or anyone else for that matter. She was nothing to it.

We were nothing to it.

With the flint spear tip secured to the hardened staff, Lucy felt a little better. At least she had something that would give her some distance and a fighting chance. Though if that thing decided to come at her, a spear probably wouldn't make too much of a difference.

What was it? Had it been a bear? No. It had antlers, but it was much too large to be an elk or deer, or even a moose for that matter.

Lucy's gaze caught the satphone which sat on top of her sleeping bag. Its bright yellow case stood out like a beacon, tempting her to call to the staff and tap out. There was a part of her that wanted to do just that. In fact, she had picked the phone up several times throughout the night with her fingers hovering over the power button.

Yet, something else stayed her hand—curiosity and determination. Lucy wanted, no, *needed,* to find out what that creature was. If she didn't, then the what-if game would haunt her for the rest of her life, and she would forever wonder if she had seen an elk and her eyes had played tricks on her.

But if it wasn't her mind playing tricks, then there was something out there. Something that large could easily kill her. Plus, the strange red fungus had her worried. Was it worth risking her life for money?

As she sat and listened, waiting for any sign of that thing—whatever it was—to come to her camp, her mind began to wander. Eventually, she remembered the plastic case she had found yesterday. Lucy dug it out of her pack and grabbed the memory card.

It took a bit, but Lucy eventually popped the card out of her GoPro and put the one she found into it. There were two video clips. The first was someone walking a trail and coming across a dead deer. A male voice let out a cry of excitement and rushed over to it. There was something familiar about the voice, but she couldn't place it.

Whoever it was got over to the deer, and their excitement faded when the camera panned across the carcass, showing it riddled with the same red moss she had seen all over the island.

"Another one... damn it!" said the voice. Then the video cut off.

A moment later, it turned on again. This time, the picture showed a nearby campfire burning big and bright. After a few seconds, a person walked into view and sat down to begin carving a spear shaft.

Lucy's breath caught in her throat. She knew this man.

It was Jimmy Haskin. He'd taken a primitive skills course from her a couple of years ago. A good student if she remembered correctly.

Jimmy looked at the camera, his face covered with tear-streaked dirt and ash.

"Hey, Sally. I just... I just wanted to say I love you, and I'm sorry."

Jimmy started crying as he spoke, wiping the tears away with the sleeve of his coat. He looked away from the camera and took a moment to compose himself.

"I'm sorry I went on this stupid show. I just thought, maybe with the money I could take care of us... take care of Henry, and give us all a better life, you know? Well, I don't know if I'll be back. If I don't, and you eventually see this, then know that I love you and Henry with all my heart. Tell Henry Daddy loves him. Tell him..."

Jimmy wiped his face again. Then he shook his head and turned the camera off.

Lucy stared at the GoPro for a bit, unsure of what to make of it all. What in the hell had spooked Jimmy so hard? Was it that thing with the antlers? Lucy put the memory card back in the plastic container and stuffed it in her backpack. She was about to grab the satphone and tap out. That video with Jimmy was the final straw.

Snap.

Lucy's eyes shot open. The sun was higher in the sky, and her fire had burned down to a smoldering pile of ash and ember. She must have fallen asleep.

Another crack came from the south of her camp, maybe 100... 200 yards away. She looked but couldn't see anything through the foliage, so instead Lucy closed her eyes and listened.

Something rustled through the brush.

Lucy grabbed her spear and sneaked toward the sound. She stuck low to the ground, choosing her steps as carefully as she could. The wind was blowing in from the side. As long as it didn't shift, whatever it was shouldn't scent her.

With the sun rising, things were beginning to warm up, but the ground was still cool enough to leech her body heat. Her heart hammered in her throat, and the lack of food and sleep combined with it made Lucy want to throw up.

The ground rose into a hill covered with boulders and some wilted brush. If her calculations were correct, whatever had made the noise was on the other side of the rise. Lucy stopped and listened.

The breeze caused some of the pines to sway and groan, as well as the leaves to rattle on the birch. Other than that, and her own breathing, it was quiet.

Lucy took a moment to steel her nerves before she began the climb up the rocks. She tried to remember what was on the other side, but her mind was fuzzy, and she couldn't remember.

"Okay..." she whispered.

Lucy crawled up the rocks, going slow and silent. She kept her head low and her ears open.

Adrenaline coursed through her body as she made her way to the top. It made her jumpy but focused. As she neared the crest, a crow landed in a tree next to her and let out a loud caw. She gasped, shying away from the bird before her brain could process what it was.

That's when the wind shifted, bringing the stench of death.

Lucy peeked around a large rock which allowed her to finally see what it was. She instantly wished she hadn't looked.

Pinned high into a pine was the top half of Matija's bloody body. His entrails trailed from his torso to the ground like a grotesque rope where several crows picked at them. The skin where his abdomen should have been was nothing more than a shredded mess. A sharp, broken branch protruded from his shoulder, holding him up.

"Fuck! Fuck, fuck, fuck, fuckfuckfuckfuckfu..." Her words became a garbled mess as she threw up bile and stomach acid all over the forest floor.

The birds eyed her from a distance but continued to pick and pull from their breakfast. Lucy grabbed a rock and threw it at the flock. A couple sidestepped, and one even flew up into the tree itself, but they continued to eat.

Anger coursed through Lucy's body, replacing fear and disgust. She hardly knew Matija, and what she had seen at the meet-and-greet didn't impress her, but nobody deserved this. With a loud yell, Lucy ran toward the tree while waving the spear around.

The birds scattered in all directions, cawing their displeasure. When Lucy stood before Matija's remains, the smell hit her hard. She gagged and dry heaved, but there wasn't anything left in her stomach.

Tears streamed down her face, mixing with sweat and grime. When she looked back at Matija, she swore he stared at her with his dead eyes.

"I'm sorry. I am so sorry. What did this to you?"

Matija didn't answer of course, but her question reignited a part of her brain. Whatever had done this could still be around—and she had just announced to everything within 1000 yards that she was here. Plus, those birds could have caught the attention of other predators. Crows meant carrion, and carrion meant food.

Lucy vowed to come back and get Matija down somehow, but she needed to return to camp and call for a pickup. She was done. No amount of money was worth dying over.

Lucy sprinted back to her camp, dodging branches and hopping over small rocks. When she finally made it back, sweat poured down her face as she took deep breaths. She scrambled into her shelter, snatched up the satphone, and tried to power it on.

Nothing happened.

Her fingers were shaking, making it difficult to hit the button, but she finally managed to mash it down.

Again, nothing.

"Fuck! Come on!"

Lucy crawled over to the black case where the extra batteries were and popped it open. The battery should have been fine. She hadn't even used the phone since she got to her location. Perhaps it was a dud battery. But all those thoughts disappeared from her brain when she opened the lid to the case. Sitting on top of all the batteries was a challenge envelope.

She looked around, trying to find who had placed it there, but nobody was in sight. She had just changed the camera battery yesterday, and the envelope hadn't been there before.

With a shaky hand, she reached out and touched the envelope, still thinking in a small part of her brain that it was just a hallucination, a figment caused by exhaustion and hunger. The heavy stock paper of the envelope brushed against her fingertips, and she snatched her hand away as if it were a viper ready to strike.

"No..."

Something screamed at her to burn the envelope, that nothing good could come from it. However, the logical part of her brain said it was only an envelope, nothing more.

Lucy took a deep breath, dropped the satphone on her sleeping bag, and grabbed the challenge. She opened it and pulled out the folded letter inside. When she read what it said, she dropped the letter on the ground and put a hand over her mouth.

Eat Matija. $100,000.

Chapter Sixteen

Trevor placed the backup battery into the satphone and tried to power it on. Just like with the first battery, nothing happened. He growled and flung the device into the battery box.

"Nothing. It's dead," Trevor said. "Both batteries! Can you believe it?"

Charlize sat on a log next to the fire, her arms wrapped around her chest. She had Trevor's sleeping bag draped across her shoulders and back like a blanket. If she heard him, she didn't let on, instead staring into the flames and at nothing at the same time.

"Do you have your phone?" Trevor asked.

When Charlize still didn't answer, he reached out and touched her lightly on the arm. She let out a scream and shied away from him.

Trevor immediately held his hands up and backed off. "It's okay, it's just me."

Charlize's eyes were wide, and her chest heaved with each breath. However, after a moment, recognition must have washed over her because her shoulders slumped, and she buried her head in her hands.

"It's okay. It's going to be okay. Did you happen to bring your satphone with you?" Trevor asked again, taking a seat across the fire from her.

Charlize shook her head but didn't say anything. Trevor cursed silently. Of course, she didn't. That was the kind of luck that had plagued him since he stepped foot on this damned island. They would have to go back and get it.

He took a moment to compose himself before speaking again. Trevor didn't want his frustration to leak through in his voice. Right now, Charlize needed comfort and security, not anger and exasperation.

"No problem. We'll just head back to your campsite and get it. There's no way that your batteries are dead as well."

Charlize pulled her head away from her hands and stared at him in horror. "No! No... We can't go back... We can't. No, no, no, no, nononononononononononono—"

"Whoa, whoa, whoa, it's okay! It's okay. You don't have to go back with me. You can stay here if you like. I can be there and back soon before nightfall."

Charlize shook her head. "You can't go there. Nobody can go there. Not after it—"

She started breathing heavily again, and Trevor feared she might hyperventilate if he couldn't calm her down. He moved over to next to her and put his arm around her shoulder.

"Hey, it's okay. It's okay. Just breathe... Take in a deep breath through your nose, then let it out of your mouth." He modeled the action a few times before she mimicked him. Finally, she calmed down.

"What happened out there anyway?"

Part of him wondered if it was a bad idea to try and drag the memories out again, especially in her state. But if he was going to hike to her camp, he wanted to know what was in store.

Trevor watched as Charlize hugged herself tighter. He was about to ask again when she started talking.

"I was patching some holes in my shelter... you know, using moss and mud. That's when I heard it—something big moving through the trees. Before I could grab my bow, it ran towards the shelter... My God, the footsteps shook the ground. It smacked the side of my shelter, and I have no idea how it didn't bust down a wall."

Charlize's lower jaw trembled, and tears ran freely down her face. She wiped them away and used the sleeve of her jacket to swipe the snot from her nose.

"Was it a bear?"

Charlize shook her head, clenching her eyes shut. "I heard it. It wasn't a bear. No way was it a bear."

"What did it soun—"

"It spoke to me. Sounded just like my mother. She told me to come quick, that she had fallen down," Charlize said.

She started gasping for air then looked Trevor in the eyes.

"That's the same thing she had yelled at me when she fell down the stairs when I was only twelve. She'd fallen and broken her femur—compound fracture."

"Charlize, I'm so sorry. It couldn't have been her though. It just couldn't."

"That's when it started banging on the walls outside. Whatever it was, slapping against the walls, screaming at me to come help. She wouldn't stop screaming. She wouldn't..."

Trevor hugged Charlize because he didn't know what else to do. He wasn't sure if what she said was true. Charlize probably believed it was true, but the mind could play tricks when deprived of sleep and food.

"I... I finally went outside to see what it was. That's when I saw it."

Trevor pulled away from her so he could look her in the eyes. "Saw what?"

Charlize opened her mouth but snapped it shut and buried her head in Trevor's chest as she sobbed uncontrollably. Her body shook.

For a long time, he simply held her, letting her cry it out. He wasn't good at these sorts of things and figured if he tried to say something, it would just make it worse. Trevor wanted to know what she saw but had enough sense not to push the issue at the moment. After a few minutes, she calmed down.

"Look, you are exhausted and just skin and bones. When is the last time you ate?"

"I don't remember. I'm so hungry though. Do you have anything to eat?" Charlize asked.

"No. But I'll go try and get us something. How about you lay down and get some rest? When I come back, hopefully it will be with some food, and we can eat."

She nodded and Trevor led her over to his bedding area, helping her get situated. He got her bundled up in the sleeping bag, and before he could say much, she shut her eyes and drifted off.

He tried one last time to use the satphone, but just like before, it wouldn't power on.

"Son of a bitch."

Trevor grabbed his supplies and headed toward the shore. He swung by his trap lines on the way hoping for a rabbit, but all the traps were just as he had left them. He hoped the fish were biting, because otherwise all they would eat was a whole lot of nothing.

Trevor made his way to the shoreline, next to the big rock where he had caught his last fish. If he could catch even one, it would be a boon. Two would be a miracle. He pulled his fishing line out of his pocket, as well as a worm he had dug out of the ground, set the bait, and then flung the hook and line out into the water.

It was a good cast, far enough out, and in a spot where he'd had some fishy action before. However, luck wasn't on his side. For over an hour he tried to catch a fish, casting the line out to different locations, trying worms and even a grasshopper, but the fish weren't buying what he had to sell today.

He thought about keeping at it, especially since he was so hungry, and he knew Charlize was as well. But at the same time, he didn't want to leave her alone for too long. She'd been through some sort of trauma, even though he didn't fully understand what had happened. Trevor didn't have to understand the details, even though he wanted to know exactly what occurred. He understood trauma well enough to know that Charlize was in a dangerous place mentally.

The wind kicked up, making it harder to cast and putting the final nail in the fishing coffin. Trevor reeled the line in by hand and put it back into his pack. With no food, he'd have to check in with Charlize, make sure she was still doing okay, and then go foraging for plants and bugs to eat. It wouldn't be as good as fatty fish-meat, but it was better than nothing at all.

As he trudged back to camp, his stomach began to cramp up. Trevor felt lightheaded and had to stop and sit down before he fell. He needed food in a bad way.

Trevor sat for about ten minutes before he finally felt decent enough to push on. When he stood, his head spun for a moment before the feeling finally faded.

"Come on, get it together," he said to himself.

His camp was just ahead, with the smoke from his campfire helping mark the location. As he neared the site, the scream of an injured squirrel tore through the air. Trevor looked around for the critter, wondering if it was coming from one of his traps, but it was closer to his camp.

In fact, it was coming from his camp.

Trevor ran back to his shelter. It was a short distance, but he was dizzy and out of breath by the time he arrived due to lack of nutrition. When he saw what was happening, he stopped and had to grab onto a nearby tree for support.

Charlize crouched on the ground in a low squat. She had a squirrel in her hands that struggled to get away from her grip. It bit her fingers, but Charlize didn't let go. Instead, she sank her teeth into the creature's back and ripped away a bloody chunk of fur.

It screamed even louder and tried to wriggle out of her grip, but she squeezed it harder and took another bite out of the animal.

Charlize looked up at Trevor, her mouth covered with blood and bits of fur. Her eyes were wide, and a crazed grin was plastered across her face.

Chapter Seventeen

Lucy crumpled the envelope and threw it into the fire. She stared at it in abject horror thinking it wouldn't burn, but after a moment, it finally caught and began to smolder. Green tinted smoke rose from the paper into the air causing Lucy to back away, as she didn't want to breathe any of that into her lungs.

Matija had been the final straw, but that envelope and its damning challenge was just icing on the fucked-up cake.

She quickly gathered her essential supplies and put them into her pack. She left the camera equipment and the satphone; it was dead anyway. Lucy then grabbed her pot and scooped some burning embers from the fire. If she could keep the embers and coals going, then making a fire when she needed to next wouldn't be too much of a hassle.

This wasn't a reality competition anymore; this was survival. Something or someone was out there killing the others, and it would only be a matter of time before it came for her. She thought of the large shape with the antlers she had seen before and shivered.

Lucy decided to head the opposite direction from where she had found Matija. If Matija had been killed to the east, then perhaps another survivalist would be to the west. As much as Lucy didn't want to hook up with the others, this was a situation that warranted teamwork and strength in numbers. Especially if there was some wild beast out there in the woods.

With the embers secured, Lucy put out her own fire. There was a small part of her that winced at the action, knowing that fires were life out here, but she also didn't want to leave it going since she didn't plan on coming back to this spot. Evading a murderous beast and trying to survive a wildfire was too much at once.

With all the preparations made, Lucy grabbed her things and headed out. She stopped just before her shelter would slip out of sight and turned to look back. There was a strange mix of emotions that washed across her. First and foremost was fear. Lucy was about to head out into the unknown, in unfamiliar territory, with *something* out there killing people. Would it come after her? How far would she have to go before she bumped into someone else?

The second emotion was exhilaration. Lucy lived for this kind of exploration. It was a part of why she joined the military. Sure, it was to escape an abusive father, but there was a part of her that yearned for the adventure the military could offer. Discovering what was around a bend or over a mountain filled her with an excitement she couldn't quite explain.

However, those emotions drained from her not even an hour into the trek. Exhaustion overwhelmed her body, and each step became harder. Dizziness plagued her, and more times than she cared to count, Lucy almost fell. One of the major fears she had was losing the coals in her pot. If she dropped that, it would be hard to get another fire going in her current state. It would be an energy expense she couldn't afford to pay.

It wasn't long before Lucy found herself climbing up a small hill to try to get a better vantage point. The hope was that she'd be able to spy smoke from a campfire to give herself a better bearing on where someone else could be.

The climb itself wasn't anything too difficult—or it shouldn't have been—but in her current state, each step was ten times as hard. When she neared the top, sweat covered her body, and she was lightheaded. Her muscles cramped and screamed at her to take a break.

Lucy found a nearby boulder to sit on and dropped her gear with a sigh. She placed the pot on the boulder next to her and watched in horror as it slid off and clanged against the rocky ground, spilling the coals out into the open.

"Fuck!"

Lucy scrambled to scoop them back into the pot, but it was too late. They had extinguished.

"No, no, no!"

Lucy tried with all her might and willpower to coax life back into the coals and embers, but they were dead. Tears flowed as a string of curses came out of her mouth that would have made a pirate blush.

After the cursing were simply tears. Frustration for being so clumsy. Frustration for being so hungry. And frustration for feeling helpless.

But if Lucy was anything, helpless wasn't it. It just wasn't part of her DNA.

"Okay, get it together. Just get another fire going..."

Lucy decided fire was the biggest priority. Without it, she could freeze overnight. There were plenty of sticks and wood around, so Lucy started gathering them up. Then, she took out her knife and began to fashion them into smaller and smaller pieces of kindling which would make it easier to get things going.

By the time she finished, the sun was on the descent. It had taken her much longer than she had hoped, but there was enough daylight left that Lucy figured she could use her ferro rod and get a fire going.

However, when she went to find her ferro rod in her pack, it wasn't there. Lucy's heart dropped into her guts as she frantically scoured her pack and pockets. Yet, after an exhaustive search, it wasn't there. What was there was a hole in her pack where the rod should have been.

Lucy wanted to cry, but she was out of tears. She wanted to lay down in the dirt and wait until someone came to get her, but who knew who or what that someone would be. Besides, she'd been in worse situations.

After taking a moment to compose herself, Lucy got up and found a stick that would work for a bow drill. Trying to get a fire going through friction would be tough. But Lucy was tough.

As she gathered the wood and prepared it, something caught her ear. Something not too far away and getting closer. The sound of *something* stepping on the rocks and coming towards her.

Randall walked down the hallway, admiring the paintings of the dark woods. A German artist named Walter Graf had painted them in 1722. Rumor had it that Graf was a nobleman who spent the last three years of his life sequestered in his bedroom, painting scenes of woods and speaking of a *thing* that spoke to him through the colors. Randall knew he had spent the last three years of his life committing unspeakable acts, mainly because Randall had pushed him towards those acts. Graf had been easy to manipulate. People like him were always easy to manipulate.

Graf died in his bedroom, reportedly torn to shreds by some animal, though there was no sign of forced entry (the guards had to bust the doors down). The paintings circulated hands many times before Ms. Thomas purchased them at auction for a hefty sum. Of course, she would never have found the paintings if he hadn't tipped her off as to their whereabouts.

As Randall walked down the hallway, he swore he could feel wind blowing across his face. It made him smile.

"Hungry, are we?"

A tree groaned, threatening to snap in one of paintings, when Randall exited the hallway and crossed the threshold into the meeting room. He hurried through the room to enter another hallway that led to Ms. Thomas' personal chambers.

Her door was shut and locked, and a large man with a neck thicker than Randall's quad stood next to the door with an MP-5 sub-machinegun slung across his shoulder. The guard nodded to Randall as he neared and opened the door.

"Thank you, Timothy," Randall said as he entered Ms. Thomas' bedroom.

The room itself was dark, as all the curtains were drawn shut. Candlelight from a dozen candelabras provided the only illumination, their flickering wicks making the light dance with the shadow in an endless waltz.

Ms. Thomas sat cross-legged in the middle of the floor, centered in a circle of different colored candles. Incense burned nearby, giving the room the cloying scent of cloves and other exotic smells.

Ms. Thomas wore a sheer black robe that left very little to the imagination. It allowed Randall to see the series of scars and tattoos across her body that were generally covered. They were symbols of power and incantations written in languages that predated the Sumerians by thousands of years. Words that most humans didn't even know existed. Randall knew what they meant, as he had taught the words to her as he etched them into her skin, and it filled his body and soul with titillating excitement.

The rash on her arm had spread as well. Deep red and angry. Randall could almost feel it pulsing with power. She was lucky to have been touched by Him.

"Do you have an update?" Ms. Thomas asked.

"He has chosen his disciple. They have left their camp and are on the move."

"Excellent. Then everything is proceeding as planned?"

"So far," Randall said. He unbuttoned his shirt and took his pants off, revealing that his body was a canvas for the arcane like Gwendolyn's was.

"Good."

Randall removed the rest of his clothes and sat down in front of Ms. Thomas. Together, they spoke, uttering words that only the wind, trees, and rocks remembered. The power rolling off Gwendolyn's naked body was delicious and full of hunger. Hunger for power. Hunger for knowledge.

It almost matched his own.

She was a conduit for His will, and while she was growing that power, Randall was siphoning it. It only took a few *pushes* with his own will and focus to get through and tap into that conduit.

The surge of energy made him buzz with life. And the best part was, Gwendolyn had no clue what he was doing. People like her never did.

It wouldn't be too long before she found out though. By then, it would be too late.

Chapter Eighteen

Trevor watched in horror as Charlize dropped the squirrel and stared at him with hungry eyes. He'd seen that look before in rabid animals but never on a human.

"Charlize?"

She cocked her head to the side but never stopped staring at him.

"Hey, you okay?" he asked.

"Hungry... so hungry."

Trevor's mouth went dry, and his leg trembled with anticipation. He thought about running, but his gut told him if he took off, Charlize would chase him down like a predator. She was a runner; he could tell by the way she moved before. He was not.

"Yeah, I'm hungry too. Maybe we can catch a fish or check my traps again. Or heck, let's prepare that critter you got there. My dad used to have a great recipe for squirrel for the backwoods. He wou—"

Charlize shuffled on all fours towards him. Trevor's breath caught in his throat, and he took a couple of steps backward to keep the distance between them.

"Whoa! Hold on! Look, let's uh... let's not do this okay?" Trevor continued slowly backing away. "Let's get some help. Maybe we can try your satphone?"

If Charlize was even listening to him, she didn't show it. She licked her lips and continued her advance. The way she moved was more animal than human.

"When I rip the flesh from bone, it makes me feel good," Charlize said.

She looked away for a moment, lost in thought. Trevor thought this could be his moment to escape, but she locked eyes with him.

"It makes me forget that I'm so hungry. Just for a moment."

"No, I get it," Trevor said. "That first bite is always the best."

"Yes!" Charlize crawled toward him. "You understand, don't you?"

No, he didn't understand what was going on with Charlize or what she was talking about. Trevor understood it made him scared, but he couldn't comprehend where *she* was coming from.

"Maybe you should stay here while I go find help," Trevor said.

Charlize stood straight, and Trevor got the sense that she was taller than before—her arms longer, fingers ready to tear. It had to be his nerves getting the best of him.

"When I rip into muscle, and the blood flows across my mouth and across my chest, it is heaven," Charlize said.

She ran her hands across her face and neck, trailing down across her breasts and over her thighs. Every movement was enticing, like a siren's call, beckoning Trevor to come closer. But everyone knew that sirens lured sailors to their death.

When she looked at him again, her eyes were full of equal parts lust and hunger. Trevor took another step back. His heel caught a rock, and he fell flat onto his back, knocking the air from his lungs. Before he could get up, Charlize was on top of him.

Her body was hot, feverish, and covered in sweat. Her musk rolled into his nostrils, and it wasn't like anything he'd smelled before. It was primal, but also alien, an acrid but somewhat sweet smell.

Trevor tried to push her off, but he was still struggling for oxygen. Charlize pinned his arms down to the dirt with ease, locking her hands around his wrists in a vise-like grip. When he tried to break free, she clamped down harder and gnashed her teeth at him.

"Charlize..." he wheezed.

Charlize moved her face next to his and then sniffed him. It was a long, drawn out drag of air which caused her to shudder.

"You smell delicious," she said. "You're a little thin, but look at all this warm meat." Charlize let go of one of his arms and ran a finger across his cheek and down his chest. Her touch made him break out in goosebumps and shudder, but not in excitement—in fear.

Trevor tried to push her off him, but she pinned his arm once again and weathered the bucks and his attempts to throw her off like a veteran rodeo champion. Charlize reared her head back and then smashed her forehead into his nose. The impact knocked the back of his skull against the hard dirt, causing his eyes to water as blood spewed out of his nose. He let out a pained cry and tried to grab his face, but Charlize still secured his wrists.

She leaned in close and licked the blood from his lips. Charlize shuddered and took a deep breath.

"Yes! Yes, that's it," she whispered. She let go of one of his arms and cupped his chin. "This is going to last a long time, and it's going to hurt."

Charlize squeezed his chin hard. He tried to scream, but the way she held his jaw made it awkward. Her fingers were more like claws, digging into his skin, tearing with a strength she shouldn't have had.

Trevor slapped at her hand to try and knock it away, but he might as well have been trying to slap a steel pipe. Charlize tightened her grip, and Trevor swore he felt something pop in his jaw. Pain unlike anything he had ever felt before ripped through his skull.

The hunger in Charlize's eyes turned to something else, something darker. She was enjoying this.

Trevor gave up trying to knock her hand away and reached around in the dirt. Finally, his fingers brushed against the cool, rough edge of a rock. He grabbed it and swung it up at Charlize's head with everything he could muster.

It connected with a heavy thud, and instantly she let go of his chin. Without thinking, Trevor bucked her up and off his body and rolled away, leaving her kicking and screaming in the dirt.

He rolled to his knees and reached up to his jaw. It was tender and sat at an odd angle. Trevor took a chance and moved it back into place with a loud pop that made him want to puke. He gave Charlize a quick glance and found her clutching her skull, blood pouring through her fingers.

Trevor wasted no more time and got to his feet, but as he started to run away, Charlize let out a wail. It wasn't a pained cry or an angry cry. It was sadness. He stopped and turned toward her, ready to fight again if need be.

She lay on the ground hugging her knees to her chest. The wound on her head bled profusely, the blood running down her skull and onto the dirt and rocks. If she didn't get it taken care of soon, she would be in trouble.

"Please..." she cried. "Please help me."

There was a timbre in her voice that kept Trevor from leaving her there on the ground. It was as if she had transformed back into the Charlize he had met back at the compound. Her eyes didn't hold the sadism and hunger they had moments ago. She seemed smaller now, unthreatening. Yet, just a few heartbeats ago, she was talking about how she was going to torture him before killing him and eating him for dinner.

"What is going on?" Trevor asked.

It hurt to talk, and his jaw made a strange clicking noise when he did. He didn't think it was broken, but he wasn't a doctor.

"I don't know," Charlize said, still lying on the ground. "I don't know."

Trevor still wanted to run as far away as he could, but where would he go? Besides, if Charlize was suffering from some sort of mental breakdown, then leaving her alone would be a death sentence.

Instead of going, Trevor shuffled over to her, dropped to his knees, and tried to stop the bleeding. Charlize sobbed and hugged him.

Trevor hoped he wasn't making a mistake, since it would probably be the last one he would ever make.

Chapter Nineteen

Lucy grabbed her spear and dashed behind a rock. She looked all around for the sound's source but couldn't see anything yet. Her heart skipped a beat when she noticed her gear still lying on the ground out in the open.

"Fuck," she whispered.

She debated whether or not to rush out and grab it when the crunch of footsteps on the rocks and dirt hit her ears.

Whatever it was, it was close. Real close.

Lucy thought about making a run for it. Perhaps she could outrun whoever—or whatever—was out there. But she dismissed that idea almost as fast as it came to her. For one, she was exhausted and malnourished. Perhaps if she were in full health, it would be an option. But the thought of sprinting right now made her dizzy just thinking about it. Besides, if it were an animal... like that thing she had seen before.

Why was it so big? Why did it have antlers?

If it was an animal, there was no way she would outrun it. Even fully rested, fed, and good to go, there just wasn't any way to outrun an animal.

Once, when she was much younger, she spent some time in Montana out in the Flathead National Forest. While she was out there foraging for berries, she had heard a large crash in the trees, and when she turned, she found two bears running at full speed through the forest. The pair covered three hundred yards in a matter of seconds and climbed up a tree as if it were flat ground. It was impressive and scary at the same time.

No, she had one choice—stay hidden and stand her ground. Lucy hoped whatever it was wouldn't smell her (the wind was in her favor) or see her. She held the spear close to her chest and waited.

For a while, nothing happened. The mountainside was quiet with only the sound of her breathing filling her ears. That's when she noticed it was *too* quiet for a mountain. Usually, there was the chirping of birds, the chatter of squirrels, or the buzz of busy bugs. But everything was silent.

It reminded her of being deployed and never knowing what was going to happen next. Everything ramped up when you stepped outside the wire. Lucy was definitely outside the wire this time. She peeked around the boulder to see if she could catch a glimpse of whatever it was but couldn't see anything.

Lucy berated herself for not going to get her things and dragging them out of sight, but she knew if she stepped out now it would be a bad idea. Yet, it was all right there. She could grab it and be back behind the rock fast.

Lucy took a deep breath to steady herself and stood.

"Lucy."

It was her brother's voice, and it stopped her in her tracks. She whipped around, fully expecting to see him lying on the ground, shot and bloody. But nobody was there. When she turned around again, something was ambling up the hill.

She dropped back to the ground and waited.

A moment later, Lucy could hear it shuffle over. It was huffing, making a strange sound that reminded her of a moose mating call, but quieter, like a low warbling moan.

The wind was in her favor, but it also meant she could smell whatever it was on the other side of the rock, and it stunk like death and rotting meat. Lucy suppressed a gag.

The odd sound stopped, and so did the shuffling. Then, whatever it was, unzipped her pack.

What kind of animal could unzip a pack? Her curiosity got the better of her, and she stole a glance from behind the boulder. It wasn't too large. Matted fur the color of cinnamon covered its body. It dug around in her pack, pulling out her supplies one by one, inspecting them carefully before flinging them away.

Lucy caught a glimpse of a gloved hand. It wasn't an animal. It was a person.

A person she could deal with.

Lucy stood and brandished her weapon before calling out. "Hey!"

The person spun around and stared at her from underneath a furred hood. His face was covered with a dirty beard and mud, but the whites of eyes stood in stark contrast. Lucy knew him.

"Burke?"

Burke stood tall as he pulled the hood off his head. His face was gaunt and his eyes sunken. The wind caught his rough-hewn fur coat, revealing a horrifically thin body.

"Lucy? Is that you?"

His voice was hoarse, and when he spoke, he stared at her like she wasn't real. When he shuffled closer, Lucy held him back with her spear. For all she knew, Burke was the one who had killed Matija.

"That's close enough," she said.

He looked around as if he were searching for something but nodded.

"Do you have any food?"

Lucy shook her head.

Burke sighed and then went back to rummaging through her belongings. What was up with this guy?

"Hey! Stop that now!"

Burke put his hands up over his head and sat on the ground. He let out another low moan like before and grabbed his belly.

"I am soooo, hungry."

Lucy didn't say anything as she circled around him and gathered up her gear. She kept an eye on him as she did, afraid he might try to jump her or something.

When she had her gear secured, she placed everything next to the boulder. "When was the last time you ate?" she asked.

"I don't know. I just know that I'm starving. I need food. Anything!"

Her rations were scarce, and she needed the calories as much as he did. But she couldn't stand to see others suffer. Lucy sighed and dug into her pockets to produce a handful of berries.

Burke's eyes went wide, and he snatched them out of her hand and shoved them into his mouth. He barely chewed them before swallowing.

"Thank you! Do you have any more?"

She thought about lying, but what was the point? "Yes. But we need to ration what we have. Who knows when we'll get more?"

Burke's face crumpled with anger, but he closed his eyes and massaged his temples. When he opened his eyes again, he wore a mask of resolve.

"Yeah, that makes sense," he said. "It's getting late. We don't want to be out when it's dark. You can come back to my camp. It isn't far, plus I have a fire going."

This should have been amazing news. It was what Lucy had wanted in the first place. She had set out to find the others and then find a way off the island. But Lucy didn't trust Burke. There was something off about him. Not that she had trusted the man much before, but now, it was different. She couldn't quite place it.

He was right. It was getting late, and the likelihood of building a fire using primitive methods wasn't encouraging.

"Okay, let's go," Lucy said. "Lead the way."

After she gathered her things, he started down the mountainside, and Lucy followed. He chose his steps carefully, testing foot placement and trying to keep quiet. Burke would often stop and look around, watching and listening. He even sniffed the air on occasion.

"What are you looking for?" Lucy whispered.

Burke stared at her, remaining quiet for a long while, as if he were mulling over whether or not he was going to tell her. Then, he asked a simple question, one that sent chills down her spine.

"Have you seen it yet?"

"Seen what?"

Lucy already knew the answer. The antlered *thing.*

A loud grunt echoed up a nearby draw, causing Burke to crouch low. Lucy instinctively followed suit. He got down on his belly and low crawled over to the edge of the hill and looked down. Then, he turned his head toward her and motioned for her to follow.

Lucy did not want to follow him, but once again, her curiosity got the better of her. She shed her pack and crawled over next to Burke with her spear by her side.

At the edge, she could see down about two hundred yards. It was a sheer drop into some nasty looking rocks, but soon thereafter, the trees ruled over the rocks. At first, she couldn't see anything but vegetation. But then it moved.

Lucy had thought it was a tree at first, but when it shifted its weight, the branches swayed in such a way that gave away its position. It wasn't a tree, and those weren't branches.

They were antlers—a mass of them stretching out behind the thing's head like an elk. It was massive, bigger than any bear or elk she had ever come across. Brown, patchy fur covered its body, but its head was bone-white, as if it were skeletal.

It took a few steps before standing upright. The thing reached into the trees and pulled a deer carcass out with one clawed hand. Then, to her amazement, it ambled off and out of sight on two legs as if it were a person.

Chapter Twenty

Trevor lost track of time as he sat on the ground hugging Charlize. He lost himself in that embrace, letting his mind stop worrying about the situation, what was going on, and all the crazy shit. There were only the two of them.

For a long while, Charlize sobbed in his arms. Finally, her cries quieted, and the only thing that came out of her was the occasional sniffle.

It had been a long time since he held another person. He had forgotten how it felt. He wished things were different and that he had made different life choices. Yet, the wishing game was just that—a game. Nothing more than a fancy and a mind exercise. Wishing didn't save lives.

People saved lives. That's what Trevor needed to do.

"Charlize, I think we need to leave."

She didn't say anything but stiffened in his arms.

"It's obvious nobody is coming, so that means it is up to us to get out of here."

Charlize still didn't say anything, but she pulled away from him, further breaking the spell. He let her go and stood, stretching his legs. A wave of dizziness washed over him, and he had to brace himself against a nearby tree or possibly fall over.

"Are you okay?" Charlize asked.

He nodded, but it was a lie. Trevor was running out of energy as his body literally ate itself to keep him moving. They both needed food, something other than raw squirrel. Just the thought of Charlize ripping the squirrel apart made him want to run and leave her behind, but it wasn't in him to abandon someone.

"Which way was your camp again?" Trevor asked.

Charlize pointed to an area laden with hills and trees. Trevor ran the numbers in his head. If they went that way, eventually they should run into some other contestants. Strength in numbers would help, plus then perhaps they could assist with keeping an eye on Charlize. But there was something that ate at him. Something Randall had mentioned during the orientation.

"There's something at the center of this island," Trevor said. He remembered seeing it from the air as they flew in. Randall had said something... what was it?

"The center of the island is off limits," Charlize said. Her voice was low and cracked.

"Yeah, I know. But why?"

It came to him then, the Von Bisping mansion sat at the center of some sort of crater or lake or something. It might be ruins, but it might hold some clues on how to get off the island.

"Look, these damn challenges keep showing up. That means that someone has to be on the island to deliver them, right?"

Charlize stared at him, her eyebrows furrowed in thought.

"Where are they staying? Probably at that mansion. That means if they got on the island, they may have a way off! Or at the very least, some sort of communication back to the mainland. Look, it's our best option. I say we pack up some gear and head that way."

"But what about the competition?"

It was clear Charlize wasn't in her right mind. She had just torn a squirrel apart with her bare hands and teeth, but she was still concerned with winning money. The real prize now was getting off the island with their lives and sanity intact.

"That doesn't matter anymore. I think if we don't find a way off this hellhole soon, it won't matter. There's something here, I know it. And it's coming for us."

Charlize stood and wiped the dirt from her pants. If it weren't for the blood and bits of fur on her mouth, she would have looked like her old self. The crazed and hungry look in her eyes was gone, replaced with determination.

"Awesome, let me pack up my stuff and we'll get going. We still have plenty of time to make some decent headway if we can get out of here within the hour."

"What can I do?"

Trevor thought for a moment before the idea came to him. "We are going to need fire. Can you figure out a way to maybe transport some of these coals with us? It will make starting a fire wherever we land much easier than getting one going from scratch."

Charlize smiled and got to work without a word. Trevor got moving as well. He packed up his sleeping bag and all the equipment he had arrived with. He decided to leave all the camera equipment behind other than one GoPro and an extra battery. Something in the back of his mind told him he needed to record this journey and what was at the ruined mansion. The world needed to know what Randall King and Gwendolyn Thomas were up to. They had to pay for their sick crimes.

He finished packing his gear and stepped out of the shelter. Charlize stood by the fire with her back turned.

"Did you get the coals ready for transport?" Trevor asked.

She didn't say anything but instead turned. In her hands was a challenge envelope. Trevor's heart sank at the sight of it.

"Where did you find that?" he asked.

She still didn't say anything. Charlize stared at him with wide eyes and a quivering lip. Trevor took a step forward and dropped his pack, and Charlize took a step back, matching him.

"It's okay. I just want to know what it says," Trevor said.

Charlize threw the envelope into the fire.

"Whoa! What the hell?"

Trevor rushed forward and fished it out of the coals just as it was catching flame. He patted the envelope until he was convinced it wouldn't burst into fire.

Charlize continued to back away from him, but he hardly noticed. Instead, he was interested in what the challenge was.

"Did you see anyone drop it off? What direction did they come from?"

Again, Charlize didn't answer. However, Trevor didn't push the matter, as he had opened the envelope and read the contents.

Kill Charlize. $1,000,000.

Randall walked down the hallway and into the operations room. Once inside, he straightened his shirt and tie. A group of technicians stood in a group near one of the desktop monitors, and the room was abuzz with commotion.

"What is going on?" Randall asked.

They turned as a group, and when they saw him, a couple of the techs hurried back to their desks. He could feel their fear, and it was exhilarating. However, there was a time to feed on emotions and a time to let people have their fun.

"It's okay, show me."

One of the techs, a portly fellow with thinning hair and curly mustache piped up. "Sir, there is... um, well, He is feeding."

"Oh, is that so? On whom?"

"It's a grizzly," said another tech.

Randall walked over to the monitor. The imagery was grainy and in IR, so he could only see black and white images. He stared at a clump of fur in the middle of the screen. It could have been a bear, but it was hard to discern any detail.

However, after a moment, the clump moved and stood on two legs. Its massive antlers branched from its skull, stretching high into the sky. With one arm, it lifted the bear—which had to weigh over 600 pounds—off the ground and into the air. The thing looked straight into the camera, as if it knew it was being watched. Two beady, glowing eyes glared at the screen with palpable malice. Its bony face was more animal than human, stretched long like an elk or moose. It still bore some facial structure similar to a person, but its teeth were sharp, and there were way too many in its mouth. It ripped a leg off the bear and tossed the body back onto the ground.

The thing tore a chunk off the leg and then strode into the forest.

"Impressive," Randall said.

"If you thought that was cool, you should see the kill video! The bear didn't even know what had hit it!" the portly tech said.

Randall stared until the smile faded from the tech's face.

"Get back to work, all of you. We are approaching the final phase. We may be lucky to witness a transference this time around!" Randall said.

The techs looked at him and each other with surprise in their eyes. The room grew louder as the workers began murmuring to one another. Randall held up a hand, silencing them.

He turned his attention to the dark-skinned tech. "What about the corrupted?"

She cleared her throat before answering. "Subject Two is nearly fully corrupted, as well as Subject Three. However, Subject Four is fighting it."

"Good," Randall said. "It's better when they fight it. It makes their fall all the sweeter."

Chapter Twenty-One

The journey to Burke's camp was a blur as thoughts raced through Lucy's mind. What was that thing? Was it the same thing she had seen previously? More than likely, but it just didn't make sense. Elk weren't that big, and they didn't stand on two feet.

Perhaps it was a bear hauling an elk carcass, but the more she thought about that, the more she didn't buy it. It was something else. Something unnatural.

Her mind was lost in a sea of could haves and should haves. She should have just stayed home and given Randall the finger when he asked her to join the show. She'd be broke but would have a higher chance of survival than being on this damned island. Now, instead of trying to scrape cash together by teaching survival classes to folks who didn't show up, she was trying to navigate a forest island with a man she barely knew all the while hoping to avoid whatever the hell that fucking thing was out there.

"Have you tried your satphone?" Lucy asked.

Burke glanced back at her and rolled his eyes. "Just a paperweight."

"Mine too."

"It's obvious that they never intended to take us off this island. This is our tomb now. We are nothing more than food and playthings for that *thing*."

There had to be more to it. Why would they risk everything to bring a bunch of people out here to die? It didn't make sense.

Lucy glanced back to where they had come from and noticed they were heading inland. Everyone's camps were supposed to be close to shore, but it wouldn't be too long before the shoreline disappeared from view.

"Where are you taking me?" Lucy asked. She gripped her spear tighter, taking comfort in its weight.

"Camp."

"No, everyone's camp was close to the water. Why are we heading toward the center of the island?"

Burke glanced back again. He had a determined look in his eyes. "I moved my camp early on because of the wind. It was getting crazy, and I just couldn't take it anymore."

Lucy tried to remember, but she didn't recall any heavy winds hitting the island since they had arrived. Perhaps this area was windier than the rest? Still, she didn't like where this was going.

"Not much further now," he said.

They hiked for another ten minutes before coming up to a patch of dead timber. Bare pines stretched up into the sky like spikes, stretching out as far as she could see. It was such an abrupt change, it took Lucy by surprise.

"What the hell happened here?" she asked.

Burke shrugged and kept walking. When he reached the line of dead trees, he turned toward Lucy and motioned for her to come close.

She was hesitant but finally walked closer to him. There was something in his eyes she didn't trust.

"Don't listen to anything in these woods," he whispered.

"What? What are you talking about?"

Burke put a finger to his lips to shush her. "Quiet, and don't listen."

With that, he turned and walked into the dead forest. Lucy watched him go, wrestling with the option of turning and running the other way. There was something about these trees that scared her. The way the shadows seemed to dance in the distance, or the way they swayed even though she couldn't feel any wind. However, there was strength in numbers, and Burke was already way ahead of her. She sighed and followed him.

Things were *off* in the dead forest. It was colder, and the sunlight didn't penetrate as hard, although it was on the descent. It was just a trick of the light, her nerves, and lack of food. Nothing more.

It was quiet in the trees. Quieter than it should have been. That's when she noticed the forest noises were gone. No chirping birds, screaming squirrels, or other such things. The forest and wild places on the earth had a voice, and if you listened, you could usually hear the general chatter and gossip of the natural world. However, this place was quiet... silent as a tomb.

At least it was at first.

Lucy tried her best to keep up with Burke, but he moved through the pines as if he were on a mission.

"Hey, wait up," Lucy whispered as loud as she dared. If Burke heard her, he didn't say anything.

"Burke!"

But he kept walking.

"Lucy."

The voice came from behind her. She whipped around, her spear held at the ready. However, there wasn't anyone or anything there.

"Who's there?" she asked.

The wind kicked up, pushing dirt and dried pine needles along the ground. The snap of a twig came from her left.

Lucy turned towards it but still couldn't see anything.

"Lucy!"

It came from behind her again. She spun towards the voice but still couldn't see anyone. That's when the sun fell behind a mountaintop and bathed the forest in darkness. With the shadows came the whispers—hundreds of voices, coming from all directions.

Lucy turned in a circle, trying to see who was talking, but there wasn't anybody there. It was hard to hear what they were saying, as the voices bled together creating a din that made her head ache.

When she tried to focus on one voice, it would disappear, only to be replaced by several more.

She dropped to her knees as tears blazed down her cheeks. "Stop it! Stop!"

But the voices did not stop. The whispers became screams, howls of pain and agony. She dropped the spear and fell to her side, curling into the fetal position. Lucy tried covering her ears, hoping it would help, but it did nothing.

Then, through it all, one voice stood out. It was her brother's voice.

"It's so dark in here Lucy, and cold. I'm hungry... so hungry."

"Stop... please! You're not him. You're not my brother," she cried.

"Just let me eat!"

"Stop it!" Lucy screamed.

The whispers did stop then. And once again, the dead forest was silent. Lucy got to her knees and looked around, hoping to find Burke, but she was alone.

"Burke?"

Nothing.

Lucy used the end of her spear to help her up to her feet when there came a noise from behind her. It was low at first, just a slight click and clack.

She froze, hoping if she stood still, whatever it was would go away. Why a simple noise so inane would make her heart skip a beat, she didn't know. But the fear was real, ingrained in her and everyone else who had heard it. Whatever made that noise wasn't just a loose branch in the wind. It was something else entirely.

The click happened again, faster this time, and closer, followed by a low growl that was so guttural it shook Lucy's spine.

Don't run from predators. That was what her grandpa taught her when she was younger. It would trigger their chase instinct. But she couldn't hold still.

Lucy ran.

She ran for her life, busting around trees and under low-hanging branches as best she could. Still, the trees were so thick that they scratched and scraped her as she ran, drawing blood. Whatever was after her gave chase.

It busted through the trees she had dodged, and from the sound of it, they didn't even slow the thing down. Lucy didn't dare look back. To lose focus now would be death. One wrong step and she knew that thing would get her.

"Join us!"

It was the whispering voices, now speaking in unison. Their combined weight of words drove into her mind like a splinter, creating jagged tears and wounds on her psyche.

Finally, she burst through the trees into a clearing, and what she saw gave her pause.

In the middle of the clearing sat a large, twisted tree that stretched high into the sky, higher than any of the others. It wasn't a pine, but something... else. Lucy had never seen a tree like this before in her life.

The trunk was massive, wider than a bus, with dark-colored bark that reminded her more of mottled skin than anything else. Its branches twisted in all directions, covered in sharp, semi-translucent thorns and leaves the same color as the red moss fungus she'd seen everywhere.

However, it wasn't what the tree looked like that gave her pause. It was what was on the tree itself.

Twisting symbols and sigils covered the base of the trunk. Lucy tried to figure out if she'd seen them before, but just looking at them for too long made her nauseous. One etching in particular caught her eye. It was of a great, antlered figure rising above a mass of people bowed in supplication. Below them all was another figure. This one was a giant worm with so many teeth it made Lucy's eyes water. Tendrils sprouted from the worm, connecting with the creature and all of its zealots. That wasn't all. Attached to an iron ring anchored into the tree about ten feet high were a set of metal chains, each ending with locking cuffs.

It was a sacrificial altar.

"Glad you could make it."

Lucy turned around and found Burke standing behind her. He had a sad look in his eyes.

"Sorry kid, but I got to feed my family."

With that, he bashed her in the head with a rock, and everything went black.

Chapter Twenty-Two

Trevor put his hands up in the most unthreatening way he could imagine, but Charlize continued to back away from him.

"Whoa, whoa, it's okay. I'm not going to hurt you. Those fuckers back at their comfy office can fuck off," Trevor said.

"No, no, no... You're going to kill me!" Charlize said.

"No, I'm not! I swear!"

Charlize obviously didn't believe him because she got up and ran. Trevor ran after her a couple of steps before a dizzy spell hit him and he almost tumbled over. He watched her run, and his heart sank when he saw which direction it was she was going.

Charlize was headed for the high cliffs nearby. Trevor's mind raced as he tried to figure out if he should go after her or not. Those cliffs were too high for his liking. Ever since the crash, he just didn't like heights. On the other hand, he couldn't let her run off alone when there was some strange animal out there killing things. It wasn't safe. Plus, in her current state, she might get dizzy like he just had and fall and hurt herself.

"Charlize! Stop!"

But she was gone. He growled in frustration and grabbed his pack and bow. They didn't have any of the coals, but there wasn't time to figure out what to do with that. He'd have to make a fire with his ferro rod if they decided to keep going. This was all assuming he could catch up with her.

Trevor moved as fast as he dared, not wanting to trip, fall, or burn out in the first bit of the chase. He'd lost sight of her, but tracking Charlize wasn't too difficult. He knew sign when he saw it, and she hadn't taken any care at all to hide where she was going. A footprint here, a broken branch there. It was obvious.

He kept calling out to her, but either she didn't want to respond or couldn't hear him. Eventually, her tracks fell in line with a game trail that led up the mountain toward the cliffs. The elevation gain rose dramatically, and it wasn't long before Trevor felt the weight of his pack dragging him down.

Jagged and rough rocks took the place of trees and bushes. The elevation pushed higher and higher, and it became a game of sorts. One foot in front of the other, ten times, rinse and repeat. Trevor put his head down and picked his way up the mountain, avoiding dangerous-looking rocks and crevices the best he could.

It was exhausting, and the sweat poured down his face. Plus, he was sure he was using way too much energy at this point. But what was the other option? Wait things out at his camp? Wait for the team to come check up on him? He was almost 100% sure they weren't coming back and had never intended to come in the first place. It was all a ruse, but he couldn't figure out what they were playing at. Why bring a bunch of people out here to die?

It got to the point where he was almost climbing now, and the sun was nearly past the peaks, making it dark and even more dangerous.

"Charlize!"

He called out, but she didn't answer, so he did the only thing he thought he could. He continued to climb.

The climb got harder and harder the higher he went. At one point, he looked behind him and down, which was something he should never have done, but he couldn't help it. When Trevor saw just how high he was, he nearly lost his grip and tumbled back down onto the rocks that would have surely killed him, or at the very least maimed him. It would have meant death either way; one was just longer and involved a lot more pain and suffering.

Trevor whipped his head forward and shut his eyes. His heart pounded in his chest, threatening to burst out at any moment. He focused on his breathing and the feel of the rocks digging into his palms. There was pain, and although slight, it was enough to pull him back to the present.

"Of course, it had to be up here. Just my luck," he mumbled to nobody.

Trevor tried to see if he could catch a glimpse of Charlize, but she was nowhere to be seen. It was at that point he started to wonder if she had come this way or if he had lost her during the pursuit. Either way, once at the top, he'd have a good vantage to scout the other side of the island or perhaps see if he could find some more camps.

Inch by inch, Trevor made his way up the mountain, until finally, he crested the rise. The sun had almost fully set, and it decorated the sky with an amazing display of oranges, reds, and yellows.

Rocks, dirt, and a few trees covered the top, though the peak was nothing like it was at lower elevations. The vantage gave him a view of nearly the entire island, including the ruins built in the center. Crumbling walls sat on a tiny island in the middle of what appeared to be a crater lake of some sort. The lake itself wasn't too large, and someone had built a wooden bridge spanning the length of the shore to the ruins. Two things stood out to him.

One, there was a small seaplane docked near the ruins, and two, there was a light coming from one of the windows of the building.

That meant someone was on the island with them and perhaps they could help them back to the mainland. At the very least, perhaps there was a radio on the plane or in the ruins and they could use that to call for help.

Trevor scanned around looking for more camps. He couldn't see any, but he did catch a glimpse of Charlize running down the hill, perhaps a half mile away from him. He couldn't believe she had the energy to run like that, as simply crawling up the mountain had drained him of almost all his reserves. Yet, neither the ruins nor Charlize running wasn't the most interesting thing. The most interesting thing he saw was a large bonfire at the base of the mountain. It appeared Charlize was running straight for it.

Randall sat at his desk, perusing data collected by the technicians. As he did, there came a light knock at his office doorway. He looked up from the information and found one of the younger techs standing with a touchpad in her hands. She wore a small, golden crucifix around her neck, and he gave a slight smile. If she knew the truth about her so-called god, it would drive her mad. No matter. People were free to believe in whatever or whoever they deemed worthy of their time and devotion. At least for the moment.

"Come on in," he said.

She shuffled over and handed him the pad. On the screen was a still image of Lucy chained to the sacrificial tree. Burke stood nearby, sharpening what appeared to be a knife, though the image was somewhat grainy.

"Excellent," Randall said. "It's coming together."

The tech nodded and gave him a half-hearted smile. He handed the pad back to her and she turned to leave. Before she left the office though, he called out.

"What about the other subjects?" he asked.

The tech turned and flipped through the pad. "It appears subject two has fully turned. However, subject three has broken out from under His influence."

Randall nodded. "Keep me informed of any changes."

The tech left the office. Once she was out of sight, Randall stood and walked over to a wall safe. He punched in the security code and opened it. Inside sat an old dagger made of knapped obsidian. It had an elk antler handle.

He reached out and brushed a finger across the stone blade, and as he did, hundreds of wormlike *things* wriggled just underneath his skin. It sent ripples of power through his body, and with that power came an intense hunger.

"Soon," he whispered. "Very soon."

Gwendolyn tossed and turned in her luxurious bed and overpriced sheets. She dreamed she was at a castle made of onyx blocks. Before her was a staircase that spiraled down into the darkness below.

She grabbed a nearby lantern which lit up with a purple glow as soon as her fingertips slid around the handle. Unsure of what was down there but also knowing she had no choice but to descend, Gwendolyn took the first step.

Down and down she went, unsure of just how far or how long she had ventured. Voices whispered from the shadows. They spoke in languages she couldn't understand. The words were those which shaped the dark corners of the universe; that much she could gather. It didn't scare her. Rather, it empowered her.

The mark on her forearm pulsed with a similar light as the lantern. It didn't itch anymore, but there was a connection there. To something. Something that was at the bottom of the pit... no, the stairs. Why did she think it was a pit?

The stairs gave way to dirt and natural stone. Sigils, runes, and esoteric symbols littered the walls, all glowing with the same violet light. Once Gwendolyn reached the bottom, she found herself in a giant tunnel. If it were not for the glowing symbols, the light from her lantern would have done little against the tsunami of darkness before her.

Gwendolyn pressed on, her bare feet bloody and raw. Each step was agony, but each step also tempted her with knowledge.

The sigils gave way to twisting, ropy tendrils that pulsed like a heartbeat. Just beneath the nearly translucent, fleshy exterior of the tendrils was a dark fluid that moved with each pulse.

Gwendolyn reached out with a shaky hand and gently slid her fingers across one of the ropy masses. It shivered under her touch, and for a flash that was only a second in length but lasted eons in Gwendolyn's mind, Gwendolyn saw.

For that moment, that heartbeat, that eternal agony, Gwendolyn was connected to Him. Connected to the infinite number of victims it drained. The memories of those people, those creatures, those *other things* she couldn't even comprehend, crashed into her mind.

The lantern died, and shortly thereafter, the light from the sigils extinguished as well. The voices stopped their damnable whispering, leaving Gwendolyn in shadow and silence.

One by one, pinpoints of lavender light sprung to life in front of her like tiny stars in the night sky, burning with passion and hunger. But then Gwendolyn understood, they weren't stars at all. They were eyes. Eyes attached to the body of a giant wormlike being, burning so bright they blinded her. But not before she saw the rows upon rows of teeth as the worm opened a cyclopean maw and a tidal wave of tendrils shot out.

Gwendolyn woke then, covered in sweat. The mark on her arm had grown in her slumber, now covering most of the appendage. The last little motes of violet light glowed just underneath her skin before blinking out. Lights not unlike those she had seen in her dream.

Chapter Twenty-Three

"Lucy... wake up."

It was her brother's voice again. Up to that point, she hadn't noticed she'd been crawling through the brush. Lucy kind of came to when his voice slithered into her ear. She looked up at the sky, and instead of seeing her old home, she found tall, lodgepole pines stretching high above her, pointing to a star-filled vista.

Lucy tried to move, but iron manacles attached to a tree trunk secured her arms. That was when she knew she wasn't back home with her brother. She was on that blasted forest island.

The crack of the bonfire grabbed her attention. Burke stood next to it, and the flames were almost taller than he was. He had his shirt off, exposing his skin to the chilly night air. Strange wounds dotted his back, akin to the stars above, but these were bloody holes. Lucy couldn't tell if it was a trick of the light and shadow, but she swore hundreds of worms or parasites wriggled just underneath his flesh.

She tried to yell at him to set her loose, but the words came out mumbled. Burke had gagged her.

Burke turned around at the noise and smiled. "Ah good, you're awake."

He came closer to her holding a large knife in his hands—blood dripping from the blade. That's when she noticed several wounds on his chest. There were three of them, oozing blood that ran down his abdomen and his pants. There were large spirals that looked more like tunnels if she stared too long, accompanied by jagged lines that could have been antlers, branches, or even lightning. She wasn't sure. They looked like the same symbols on the tree.

Burke looked at her, then glanced down at the knife before letting out a hearty laugh. "Don't worry about this," he said and wiped the blade on his pants leg before putting it back in the sheath. "It's not for you. No, you're for Him."

Lucy tried to talk, but once again, the gag did its job. Burke reached up and took it off. "There you go. That should be better."

Lucy stretched her jaw a little, working it open and closed before speaking. "Let me go, now."

"I'm afraid I can't do that. Soon, He will be here."

"Who?"

"The Devourer. Avatar of the Worm. The Endless Hunger!" Burke said the last bit and raised his hands into the air as if praising God.

"Hey! Listen to me. I don't know what's up, but you need help. You're hurt, bleeding, and I think you might be sick. Just let me down and I can help you." It took all of Lucy's willpower not to scream and yell, but something told her that wasn't the best course of action.

He looked at her with a blank expression. Then that wry smile crept back onto his face again. "I'm afraid not. I have a job to do. So do you."

He walked back to the bonfire.

"Burke, you sonofabitch! Let me go!"

He turned toward her again, and for half a second, the moonlight caught his eyes, and they glowed like those of a cat. "You have a lot more fight in you than Matija did. That's good. He likes that kind of energy."

Lucy struggled against the chains, but even though they were rusty, they were still solid. Burke smiled as she fought and kicked, watching her with the same amusement one might watch a child playing with building blocks.

Lucy gave up when she realized there was no way to get free. "Please, Burke, let me go."

He shook his head. "No can do. Only He can do that."

"Come on, this isn't funny anymore!"

Not that it was funny to begin with. Burke shook his head again and turned back toward the bonfire, throwing another piece of wood onto the pile.

A strange growl came from the distance. At first, Lucy thought it might be a bear, and the idea of a huge grizzly finding her secured to a tree was terrifying. But there was something off with the growl. It was deeper and had a different resonance than any bear she had heard. Plus, there was a strange hollowness to it.

From the same direction came the thundering step of something big. Branches snapped as it moved closer and growled again. Lucy tried to see what it was, but the noise came from behind her.

Burke dropped to his knees and bowed onto the ground.

"I have brought you a worthy sacrifice!"

The thing moved closer, branches and twigs snapping, until it was right behind her. Even though the wind was blowing across her in a different direction, the thing was close enough that its stench burrowed into her nostrils.

It stank of death, but also something else. Earth. Like freshly dug dirt.

Lucy gagged and tried to keep from throwing up, but ultimately, she couldn't. Bile crawled up her throat and out onto the ground in front of her. Part of her was happy she couldn't see what was behind her, but a part of her wanted to see... *needed* to see.

"Burke! Let me go you piece of shit!"

The flames of the bonfire wavered, as if the pressure had changed. A moment later, Lucy's ears popped, and she thought her eyes might bulge right out of their sockets. Yet, as fast as it happened, it left.

The tree she was secured to shook. Lucy looked up to find a clawed hand slowly reaching around. The hand was massive, twice as big as any human's hand she had ever seen and covered in semi-translucent skin. The fingers were bony, long, nearly eight inches in length and capped with grimy talons that looked like obsidian.

Tears ran freely down her face, and Lucy did everything she could to stay still and quiet now that it was literally right behind her.

Burke looked up, and his smile turned into an expression of fear. He stood and opened his arms wide.

"Please, I did what you wanted," Burke said.

The thing growled, low and deep. It vibrated the tree and Lucy's chest at the same time. She tried her best to make herself small and invisible, though she knew it was a waste of time. That thing, whatever it was, could easily tear her apart.

But it wasn't after her. Not yet.

Burke's eyes went wide as he turned to run, but it was too late. A long bony arm reached out and grabbed him by the shoulder. Its talons punctured skin, causing blood to spray into the air like a sprinkler.

Burke let out a pained scream as the thing pulled him back and out of Lucy's field of view. The sounds of a struggle filled Lucy's ears, followed by a sick, wet crunch. A second later, Burke's headless body hit the dirt next to her.

Lucy screamed and fought against her chains with all her strength. She knew at any moment the thing would come for her, and she would be nothing but a body in the forest as well.

To Lucy's unbelieving eyes, Charlize crashed through the trees on the opposite side of the fire. She skidded to a halt and looked above Lucy at the trees and let out a scream before fainting and falling to the ground.

The crunch and grind of that thing chewing on Burke's head made Lucy sick to her stomach. It reached out and grabbed Burke's body, dragging it away. Tears fell freely from Lucy's eyes as she contemplated what was about to happen. At least she would finally be reunited with her brother.

Then, the rustle of brush sounded and Trevor stepped out of the forest. He looked at Charlize with concern before locking eyes with Lucy. A look of confusion crawled across his face. Lucy figured he must be wondering why she was chained to a tree. His gaze wandered behind her, and the confusion quickly turned into pure horror.

The thing behind her growled again. It must have noticed Trevor.

Trevor nocked an arrow and shot. It was a quick shot, but it must have hit the mark because the creature howled in pain before it barreled away, snapping trees and branches as it went.

For a moment, Trevor stood there, staring into the trees before turning his attention back to Lucy. He pointed with his bow into the forest before saying, "What the fuck?!"

Chapter Twenty-Four

Trevor's entire body trembled as he tried, and failed, to nock another arrow. He didn't dare take his eyes off the patch of wilderness he saw that *thing* slink off into, dragging Burke's body along as it went.

What was it? It was big, nearly fifteen feet tall, though that didn't even give the creature justice, as it had been hunched over. Never in his life had Trevor ever encountered such a thing.

His mind tried desperately to come up with a logical explanation. It was a bear with a dead elk carcass stuck to its back. Or maybe it was an elk that had somehow mutated? The color of its eyes though... it stuck out more than anything. A light purple glow. And it's hide was a ruddy color that didn't match any other creature he was familiar with.

The tinfoil hat-wearing conspiracy nuts always talked about chemicals in the sky. Maybe that was it? But try as he might, he couldn't explain it. The thing had been bipedal and its head was more skull-like, looking somewhat like an elk's skull, but different. Longer, with rows of sharp teeth that looked like they could rend flesh with ease. And the eyes... The thing's eyes would haunt him forever.

They had been red, catching the light of the flame and almost glowing. Or were they purple? Already, Trevor's mind was racing to make sense of and twist the facts into something more palatable for his sanity to digest.

There was a faint screaming in the back of his mind. Trevor wondered if perhaps it was his own voice, but he finally looked away from the far trees and found Lucy manacled to a closer one. As he shifted focus, the screaming got louder and became clear.

"Get me down, Trevor!"

Hearing his name snapped him out of it. He jogged over to her and examined the manacles. They were old and made of iron.

"Just a second," he said.

Looking around, he found the keys on the ground, partially covered with dirt. He let out a sigh of relief, as he wasn't sure if he could have opened the locks without them. Although the iron was rusted and aged, they opened easily enough.

Lucy stepped away from the tree, rubbing her wrists with a pained expression on her face.

"What the fuck was that?" Trevor asked.

Lucy looked past the tree into the woods. "I don't know. I don't want to know. What I do know is we need to get the fuck off this island before it comes back."

Trevor nodded in agreement but walked over to where the thing had been standing. He clicked on his headlamp and searched the area. It took a moment in the darkness, but he finally found what he had been looking for.

Blood.

He crouched down to examine it. Whatever it was, it could bleed. The blood was dark, almost black in color, and at first, he thought maybe there were tiny grains of rice in, as there were dozens of white little dots. Trevor got on his hands and knees to get a closer look. The white things were odd, not rice, but something else.

One of them moved.

Then the rest wriggled and writhed in the blood.

They were worms.

"Fuck me," he said under his breath. "Fuck this place."

He turned to find Lucy going through Burke's gear. She rifled through his backpack, flinging some things away into the bushes while pocketing other items. Then, she grabbed her pack and spear.

"Where are you going?" Trevor asked.

"Away from here," Lucy replied.

Charlize moaned. She rolled onto her side before propping herself up on her elbow. "Where..."

"Whoa there, take it slow," Trevor said and rushed over to her. He helped her off the ground and got her seated on a nearby log.

Lucy dug a mason jar full of water out of Burke's pack and handed it to Trevor. He took it, then held it out to Charlize.

"Here, take a drink," he said.

Charlize stared at him with a pained expression. She looked at Lucy, the bonfire, then to the tree with the manacles. Trevor put the mason jar into her hands.

"You need to drink. It's okay. We're okay," he said.

"For now," Lucy said. "We need to move before that thing comes back."

"Nowhere is safe," Charlize said. "It will find us, no matter where we go. It will hunt us down and eat us. Or worse!"

"We can't stay here!"

Charlize and Lucy continued to argue, their voices becoming louder as one tried to talk over the other. Trevor wasn't listening to them anymore. They were background noise.

His mind raced with what had gone on up to this point. He wanted to come up with a foolproof plan, something that would get them back to safety. As much as he wanted a different option, there was only one in his mind.

"The ruins," he said.

The pair continued to argue, oblivious to him.

"Hey! The ruins!" Trevor said, projecting this time.

Both Lucy and Charlize stopped talking and looked at him. When he had their attention, Trevor continued.

"When I was hiking earlier, I had a good view of the old castle on the lake. It looks to be in bad shape, most of it anyway. But I did see a light on in one of the windows. Plus, I saw a sea plane there. Maybe we can get help there because it is obvious nobody is coming to help us here."

"That thing will find us out there, and it will kill us!" Charlize hissed.

"It will find us and kill us regardless. At least this way we may have a chance," Lucy said.

Trevor nodded. "We arm up. We prepare. Now that we know what we're dealing with, we have a chance. Look over there," Trevor said and pointed to the worm-infested blood. "My arrow hurt it. It can bleed. And if it bleeds, we can kill it."

Lucy shot him a disapproving look.

"What?" Trevor asked.

"Really? If it bleeds, we can kill it? I bet you've been waiting most of your life to say that line," Lucy said.

Trevor laughed for the first time in a long time. "Maybe. But it doesn't change the fact that we can hurt that thing. So, we arm up, make our way to the ruins, and find a way off this fucking island."

They got to work getting everything prepared. It took them a good hour, as Trevor was suffering from severe hunger pangs. From a look at the other two, he could only figure they felt the same. Lucy was wobbly on her feet, and Charlize had to sit down and take a breather every five minutes or so. They needed food in a bad way. Trevor's stomach growled as if it had read his mind.

They split the gear as best they could. Charlize was too weak to draw a bow properly, so they gave her a spear and a knife. Trevor took his bow and grabbed a spear made from a fire-hardened branch. It was better than nothing. Lucy had her spear as well as Burke's bow.

They didn't find any food in the camp and were debating whether or not they should try to procure something to eat before heading out when the forest went silent. Charlize had been the first to notice. She looked around with wide eyes and then snapped her fingers to get Trevor and Lucy's attention.

"What?" Trevor asked.

She put a finger to her lips and clutched the spear so tight her knuckles went whiter than paper. Trevor looked around as well, the uncanny sense that something was watching him heavy on his back. He slowly nocked an arrow and listened.

At first, the only sound was his breathing and the thump of his heart. But then he heard it, so quiet at first he thought his mind was playing tricks, but then moments later, it happened again. A footfall.

Trevor turned toward the sound and steeled his mind for what was about to happen. He told himself to aim for the heart. Perhaps if they could hit the creature in the heart or through a lung, they could stand a chance.

Something scraped across branches, just out of sight. Trevor did his best to calm his nerves, breathing in and out slowly, but it did little to stop the adrenaline from coursing through his veins.

Trevor tried to imagine just how tall the creature was, and kept his eyes pinned on that height. He was so focused that he nearly missed it when Hank came stumbling through the trees.

"Jesus Christ!" Trevor said. "I nearly shot you!"

Hank stared at him with wide eyes. He bled from dozens of tiny scrapes and scratches that decorated his face. His lips were chapped and cracked, and his clothes were barely holding on, full of rips and tears.

"Water?" Hank asked.

Charlize held out the mason jar half-full of water with a shaky hand. Hank rushed over, nearly causing Charlize to drop the jar, but he snatched it away and down the liquid like a madman.

"Where did you come from? Where's your camp?" Lucy asked.

Hank finished the water and pointed back behind him. "Back there about a day's hike away."

"Have you seen it?" Charlize asked, getting closer.

Hank stopped drinking the water and wiped his mouth. He nodded. "Yeah, I've seen it. Saw it feeding on a dead deer about three days ago. Thought I was going nuts. But I saw it. It looked up at me, and I swear to God it smiled right at me. Took off running after that."

"What about your brother?" Trevor asked. "Have you found him?"

Hank finished off the water and handed the jar back to Charlize. He shot Trevor a cold gaze. "Yeah, I found him. What was left of him."

Chapter Twenty-Five

Lucy hadn't slept much that night. It was cold, even with the fire going, and the hunger pangs were overbearing. As soon as the sun started to crest the horizon and light up the sky, she gathered her gear.

The others stirred and began moving about at the same time. Perhaps they hadn't slept well either. How could they? Knowing what was out there waiting for them, it would be a miracle if any of them slept at all in the coming weeks.

"So, what's the plan?" Trevor asked.

"Like we discussed last night, we head to the ruins. By my calculations, they should be over that rise," Lucy said and pointed to a set of rocky mountains in the distance.

"Shit," Trevor said, almost a mumble. But Lucy's hearing was uncanny, and she picked it up clear as day.

"Everything okay?" she asked.

Trevor let out a nervous chuckle as he stuffed his backpack with the necessities. "Yeah. It's just that I'm not the biggest fan of heights. Plus, I don't know if I have the energy to make another climb."

Lucy studied the mountains again. They were tall, but it looked like there were ways up it. Besides, trying to find a way around could possibly burn more energy than they could afford, not to mention it could take much longer than they had time for.

"No other way. That way is the quickest," she said. "It's okay to be afraid. It's what keeps us alive. Fear can drive us. Use that energy and turn it into something useful."

"You afraid of anything?" Trevor asked, eyeing the mountains.

"Of course. I'm afraid of the dark," Lucy said. *Because that's when the voices start talking.* She didn't mention that part.

"Afraid of the dark? What are you, in elementary school?" Hank asked.

A tingle ran up Lucy's spine, and her initial response was violence. Especially when she saw the stupid look on Hank's face as he sat on a nearby log drinking water. She'd seen that look before. It was a mask bullies wore to act tough. However, she'd seen it enough times to know that Hank was scared shitless on the inside. He was just good at putting on a brave façade. Instead of punching Hank in the throat, she took a different approach.

"When I was younger, my dad wasn't what you would call a stellar example of fatherhood. He thought he could pray away the queerness from my brother and me. When the praying didn't work, he turned to other means—violent ones. I bugged out as soon as I could. Joined the military and finally found a spine."

Knowing where the story was headed caused tears to brew just behind her eyelids. Lucy wiped her face and pretended to mess with her pack. When she looked up and found everyone staring at her, she continued.

"My brother wasn't so lucky. He was younger. I thought I couldn't take him with me, thought maybe he'd be okay for just a few more years while I found my feet and made a new home for us. I was wrong.

He shot himself with my father's 1911. Sometimes, when it's dark, I can hear my brother's voice."

"Jesus…" Trevor said. He walked over and placed a hand on Lucy's shoulder. "That is horrible, and I'm sorry."

The mask on Hank's face slipped, and for just a moment, he had a look of compassion in his eyes. Then, that compassion turned to something else. He opened his mouth to say something but must have thought better about it and instead gathered his gear.

"Hey, I'm worried about Charlize," Trevor whispered. He nodded to the side. Lucy followed the motion and found Charlize sitting on the ground with her back against a tree. She had a thousand-yard stare in her eyes.

"I'll go chat with her," Lucy said.

"Do you think we should leave her here? I don't know if she can make it a hundred yards from camp let alone up and down an entire mountain."

Lucy gave Trevor a weak smile. "People can do amazing things when they put their mind to it. Let me talk with her and see how she's doing."

Trevor nodded and ambled over to the fire pit. There wasn't a flame, but the coals were still smoldering and putting off heat.

Lucy grabbed some water and shuffled over to Charlize. "Hey, you doing okay?"

Charlize looked up at Lucy. Her eyes were glassy and unfocused. She didn't say anything. Lucy handed her the water, waiting for Charlize to reach up and take it. Finally, Charlize grabbed the cup and took a sip.

"There you go, that's the trick. What is it they always say, hydrate or die?" Lucy said with a forced smile. In this place, they were likely to die even well-hydrated. That thing, whatever it was, probably didn't care. "Do you think you can make a hike today?"

Charlize took another sip of water and nodded.

"Okay then, let's get moving. We need to make headway before it gets dark."

Lucy had no idea if that thing cared about the light or not, but in her mind, it made sense. Growing up, her parents always warned her about heading out into the wilderness in the dark. That's when the predators came out. Her mom used to tell her to watch out for the Sasquatch. Said if you weren't careful, he'd come snatch you up.

When Lucy got older, she stopped believing in those fairy-tales—stories meant to keep her out of danger mainly. But now, who knows? Maybe there were strange things out there in the shadowy corners of the earth.

They packed everything up, doused the fire, and headed out. It was slow going. Each step took effort, since Lucy hadn't had anything substantial to eat in quite some time. Things got worse when they started going up the hill.

"Wait, I need a minute," Trevor said. His face was red, covered in sweat, and he had to steady himself against a tree before sitting down on a fallen log. "Just a minute, please."

Lucy dropped her pack and stretched her back. A couple of vertebrae popped, and she couldn't tell if she felt better or worse. Charlize stopped and stood, looking all around with wide eyes. She hadn't said a word since that morning. Lucy was worried about her, as she looked like she was in a state of shock or something. They needed to get her to a hospital.

Hank brought up the rear and plopped down next to Trevor.

"Hoo buddy, this is tougher than bison hide," he said with a fake grin.

Lucy scowled at the man and put a finger up to her mouth. "We need to be as quiet as possible. We don't know if that thing is out there."

Hank shrugged and dropped his pack. He took a big swig of water and wiped his face.

"What if it is out there? What if it's watching us right now, waiting for the right moment to strike?" Hank asked.

"Look, we can play the 'what if' game all day long, but it's just a waste of time and energy. We need to get somewhere safe before it gets dark," Lucy said.

"Right, because you're scared of the dark. So, we're going to kill ourselves to find a safe place here—that doesn't even exist—so you can feel comfortable?" Hank asked.

Lucy's blood boiled. She'd had enough from Hank. But before she could say anything, Trevor stepped between them.

"Hey, lay off man," Trevor said. "I know this fucking sucks, but arguing with one another and fighting all the way is for sure going to get us killed. If we want to get out of here, we need to work together. So, either shut your fucking mouth and start helping, or go your own way."

Hank stood and took a step towards Trevor. His eyes raged as he clenched his jaw tightly. Trevor stood his ground, his hand balled into a fist. Lucy watched the pair and quietly pulled her knife. She could tell from the way Trevor stood that he wasn't much of a fighter, while Hank had an air about him. He'd been in a tussle or two in his time.

Lucy gripped the knife tight—she wouldn't let it come to a brawl. She'd end it before it got to that point. The thought of slipping her knife between his ribs and into his heart filled her with fire. The way the blood would run out over her hand... how it would taste.

Lucy shook her head, and the thoughts disappeared but left a nasty aftertaste in her psyche.

As if someone had flipped a switch, the tension congealing around them dissipated. Hank turned and put his hands up.

"Have it your way, then."

He lumbered back to his gear and plopped down on the ground with a sigh. Trevor let out a breath and turned toward Lucy. His eyes caught the blade in her hand, and he gave a look that asked, "Really?" Lucy shrugged and put the knife away. It wouldn't be the first time she killed someone.

They rested in silence for a few minutes, eating a couple of bolete mushrooms Lucy had found and cooked earlier, as well as a handful of Oregon grapes.

Hank hugged his knees to his chest and stared off into the distance.

"I have a fear as well," he said. It was just above a whisper.

Lucy and Trevor looked over at him while Charlize stared at the ground. She braced herself for some stupid answer but didn't say anything.

"Bugs... Well, worms specifically. When I was younger, I was out in the woods with Emmett. We were at hunting camp with my dad and uncles. Emmett and I were too young to pack a rifle ourselves, but it didn't matter. We just liked being out there with the family.

"Well, Emmett and I were dinking around when the wind shifted and brought this god-awful stench our way. You know, the kind when an animal has been dead awhile and left out to rot."

That got Charlize's attention. She perked up and looked directly at Hank with a hungry look. Lucy had regrets about bringing her and even Hank along.

"It didn't take long to find it. Dead elk, been there maybe a couple of weeks. Lord almighty it stunk to high heaven! Being the curious little shits we were, we got as close as we could to get a better look at the carcass. I think that was the first time I'd ever been so close to something dead. I mean, sure, I'd been there when my dad had gut fish, or even other big game, but this was different. This was natural.

"Well, brothers will be brothers, I guess. Emmett shoved me when we got close, and I fell right into it. I don't mean on it, I mean, *in* it. Thousands of maggots and slimy crud covered me."

Hank scratched his arms and stared at the ground.

"I can still smell it sometimes... can still feel those little things crawling all over my body."

"Jesus," Trevor said.

"Nope. Wasn't J.C. that day. It was my asshat of a brother," Hank said. He shook his head and stood. "Guess we best get going before it gets dark, eh?"

Hank gave Lucy a weak smile and winked. She couldn't tell if he was trying to be nice or was simply still in dick mode. She gave him the benefit of the doubt this time, as it took guts to backtrack and get vulnerable with everyone.

It was late afternoon when they finally crested the rise. They had taken it as slowly as they could, but they were all covered with sweat. But thoughts about how tiresome it had been dissolved when Lucy looked into the valley below.

There was the crater lake with the ruins. And just like Trevor had said before, there was a small plane. That was their ticket out of there. Not only that, but smoke wafted lazily from one of the stone chimneys.

Somebody was home. Somebody with answers.

Chapter Twenty-Six

Trevor's foot hit an exposed tree root, causing him to stumble forward. He almost fell on the ground but caught himself on a nearby tree.

"You okay?" Lucy asked.

"Yeah, just had a dizzy spell is all." It wasn't a lie either. He'd been fighting waves of lightheadedness for the last couple of hours. Lack of food coupled with the strenuous hike had to be the culprit, not that it really mattered. They hadn't come across anything edible since they started the downhill trek.

There weren't any mushrooms except strange, rosy-colored ones that seemed to pop up around the base of dying pines. Trevor had never come across any mushrooms like that before, and when he asked the others, they had never seen them either. They were small, about the size of a quarter each, and grew in clusters of six to ten. They glistened in the sun as a foul-smelling gel oozed out of the bottom of the gills. They stunk to high heaven too, like a deep, meaty rot that you could taste. It was the kind of smell that lingered well after encountering it.

Most of the plant life was dead or dying, and it seemed to be getting worse the closer they got to the bottom of the hillside.

The thought of flying the plane put butterflies in Trevor's stomach. He was fully capable, but just thinking of cruising through the air again made him want to throw up and got his heart thumping faster.

The wind shifted, picking up in intensity as it blew across Trevor's face. It would be winter soon. In fact, Trevor was surprised it hadn't snowed yet. He pulled his coat tighter about him, but his lack of fat reserves was obvious. The only thing keeping him from shivering was the hiking. He knew as soon as they stopped, the chill would set into his marrow. Yet, it wasn't the cold that made him pause. No, the wind brought something else with it. The stink of death.

Trevor stopped to sniff again, and the others stopped behind him. The stench was coming from off the game trail they were using to hike down.

"You smell that?" Trevor asked Lucy as she walked up beside him.

She scrunched her nose and nodded.

Trevor nocked an arrow and used his nose to try and home in on the odor. Lucy and the others followed behind him, but at a distance. Whatever it was, it was past the point of edibility, but maybe, just maybe, there would be a predator around he could harvest. Just the thought of cooked meat made his mouth water.

He crept through the pines, careful where he put his feet so as not to break a twig or scrape a rock. With the wind in his face, if there was something over there, it wouldn't smell him. If he was quiet enough, it wouldn't hear him.

Up ahead was a mass of deadfall as far as the eye could see. Dead and fallen trees littered the landscape. Also up ahead was the source of the scent, as it had gotten much stronger as he walked up to the deadfall.

Trevor glanced back at the others and nodded toward the fallen trees. Lucy nodded back.

He slowly dropped his gear except for his bow and a couple of arrows. Without the weight of the pack, he would be able to move faster and quieter. Years of experience in the backwoods helped him navigate through the maze of dead timber. It was slow going, but in this case, slow was key.

Up ahead, the landscape rose slightly, making it harder to travel. Trevor was committed at this point though. By the time he was near the edge of the rise, sweat beaded on his forehead even though he had taken it easy. The stink was so bad, he had to cover his nose and mouth with an arm, or it was possible he could throw up, which would make things even worse.

Finally, he crested the ridge and found the source. Trevor couldn't believe his eyes.

In front of him was an open meadow near a creek. Dozens of animals lay on the ground in various states of decay. Deer, rabbit, elk, and even a cougar rotted in the clearing. Flies buzzed and maggots squirmed. Chunks were missing from the animals, as if something had been eating them. More of that red moss clung to the wounds on the carcasses like a fuzzy growth. However, that wasn't what made his mind crack ever so slightly.

There weren't just dead animals here; there were live ones. A pair of rabbits chewed on the corpse of a squirrel, fighting for the last few scraps of meat from its tiny body. They yanked and pulled until the squirrel ripped in half.

A doe stepped out into the clearing, found a nearby buck carcass, and ripped a piece of rotten meat from its haunch. All the animals were gaunt and malnourished, like thin, skeletal husks wrapped in mangy fur. There was something else about them too, something about the way they moved. Trevor had spent a lot of time hunting and was familiar with prey animals and predators, and these animals, that by all laws of nature should have been prey, moved like they were predators. It was hard for him to pinpoint, but deep down in his heart, he knew it to be true.

There was no way he was going to try and kill one of those animals. Just the thought of getting close to one of them made his skin crawl. Trevor slowly backed away, but as he did, his jacket caught on a sharp branch on the deadfall, and it snapped.

In unison, the animals looked up from their meals and stared at him with bloody maws. One of the rabbits hopped closer, and Trevor readied his bow, not to harvest the creature, but in self-defense.

Now, closer, it gave Trevor a better look. Blood and gore matted its fur. What was once snow white was pink, red, and black. Long strands of twisted fur seemed to sway in the wind as it took a few more hops.

Trevor's jaw began to tremble. It wasn't hair at all.

They were worms. Long worms wriggled and writhed from within the rabbit, bursting forth from its skin and reaching toward Trevor's direction like a mass of nightmare appendages. The rabbit screamed, taking jerky hops closer to Trevor, its screams sounding like an injured child boring into Trevor's ears.

He turned and ran back to the group as fast as he could. As he did, the other forest animals joined in the rabbit's screams, filling the forest with a chorus of pain and hunger.

Lucy saw him coming and looked at him and then behind him with wide eyes.

"What is it? What did you see?" she asked.

Trevor, unable to speak, only shook his head and motioned for the others to run. With everything that had happened so far, they didn't hesitate to join him, and they ran, leaving the wails behind.

He ran until his lungs screamed for oxygen and his legs became wobbly. He fell to the ground in a heap and threw up what little bile he had in his stomach, dry heaving until he couldn't see due to the tears in his eyes.

What were those things? What was happening? Those questions swam in his thoughts as Trevor's stomach lurched again and again.

Something touched his shoulder, and Trevor tried to scream but couldn't. Instead, he spun around onto his back and crab-walked away from what he thought was one of those creatures coming after him.

He found Lucy kneeling on the ground with her hands in the air.

"It's me! It's just me," she said.

Trevor wiped his mouth with the sleeve of his jacket and came away with a long string of gooey vomit. The others popped out of the trees a moment later. Hank looked behind him as he leaned against a tree. Charlize's face scrunched in pain, and she sat down on a nearby rock.

"They w-whe-the-they-the-whe..." Trevor tried to say.

"Slow down, it's okay. I think we're safe for the moment," Lucy said.

Trevor tried to control his breathing, but each breath came in ragged gasps. His lungs burned, and the coppery taste of blood tinged the back of his throat.

"There were animals... but they weren't," Trevor said when he could finally muster his voice again.

"What do you mean they *weren't*? What kind of nonsense is that?" Hank asked. "Why the fuck did we just sprint through the woods like a bunch of goddamned kids?"

"Not helping," Lucy said.

Trevor did his best to explain what he had seen. How there were dead animals and others there too eating the dead. How the red moss had taken them over—and the worms. Oh God, the worms...

When he finished, the others were speechless. Lucy constantly looked back toward the trees in the direction they had run from. Hank rubbed his temples and paced in circles, all the while muttering to himself. Charlize continued to stare into the forest.

At this point, it was getting close to the evening. Now that they were at a lower elevation, Trevor didn't know for sure how close they were to the ruins, but it couldn't be much farther. One thing he did know for sure was that they needed to keep moving.

"Come on," he said. "We need to go. It will be dark soon. And they mostly—"

Lucy held a hand up. "If you quote another movie, I swear to God..."

They continued hiking. Sometimes a strange growl or noise would cause them to stop, but for the most part, they trudged forward with manic desperation. The sun had begun to set, and the temperature was dropping fast now that the light was retreating.

Trevor lost the trail several times but did his best to keep them oriented in the right direction. His compass was acting funny though, spinning in circles at times. Other times, it would point north, only to point south the next time he'd peer at it. As the sun finally set, he realized they weren't going to make it to their destination.

"I think maybe we should stop here and start a fire," Trevor said.

"Damn straight!" Hank said and dropped his pack.

Lucy shot the man a toxic look and then got closer to Trevor. "Do you think it's safe to stop here?"

Trevor shrugged. "Here, over there, in the ruins—it's all the same, really. I think our best bet is to make a big fire and th—"

Before he could finish his statement, Charlize let out a loud moan of pain and dropped to her knees. She clutched her stomach as she doubled over.

Trevor and Lucy rushed over to her.

"What's wrong?" he asked.

"It hurts!" Charlize said through her teeth.

"What hurts?" Lucy asked.

Charlize dropped into the fetal position and screamed. She writhed on the ground clutching her abdomen.

"What the fuck?" Hank asked. "What the fuck is wrong with her?"

"I don't know," Trevor said. He reached out and placed a hand on her shoulder, and Charlize screamed even louder, causing him to jerk away.

"Make it stop!" she screamed. "Make it stop!"

Lucy pulled him away to the side. "I think we need to find her some food. It might be really bad hunger pangs or cramps or something."

Trevor wasn't so sure. He'd had stomach cramps before, but nothing like that. This was something else.

"Holy shit, what the fuck is happening to her!?" Hank shouted.

Trevor looked past Lucy to Charlize. She was still on the ground but had pulled her jacket and shirt up, exposing her belly.

Her stomach was bloated, as if she'd drank or eaten way too much. However, there was something else happening. Something that made Trevor's skin crawl when he flashed his headlamp her way.

Charlize sat on the ground clutching her belly. She screamed and began to claw at herself, as if she were scratching a horrendous itch. Trevor watched in horror as Charlize dug bloody furrows into her gut. Blood poured between her fingers and onto the ground, but there was more.

Long, spaghetti-like worms burst forth from the wounds and swayed in the night air. Bone white in color, they reached out, probing for food.

Charlize looked down at her mid-section in horror and screamed. Hank backed away from her, muttering something about his brother and the maggots. Lucy scrambled back as one of the worms extended toward her. Trevor could only stare in horror, trying to process what he was witnessing.

Finally, Charlize stopped screaming. She looked at worms, then up at Trevor.

"I don't need help anymore. I just need to eat. Soooooo hungry," Charlize said.

She started to get up but was a little wobbly on her feet and fell back to the dirt.

"I don't think you should move," Lucy said.

"I don't think you should move," Charlize mimicked. "Move. Don't think you should move. Don't move. Don't move."

Charlize got to her hands and knees, and the worms writhed and squirmed, twisting around one another, slick with her blood and stomach acid. With a shaky lunge, she got to her feet, rushing forward until she hit a nearby tree. Then she turned, staring at Trevor with a crooked smile. Her eyes caught the light of the headlamp, glowing like a cat's.

"Aren't you a fine piece of meat," Charlize said.

Then she ran straight at Trevor.

Chapter Twenty-Seven

Lucy watched, frozen in place, as Charlize ran straight for Trevor. Trevor must have been just as shocked because he didn't move until she slammed into him with a heavy thud. They both hit the ground hard, and Trevor rolled away from Charlize as she kicked and scrambled.

Charlize moved with staccato jerks as she tried to find her feet. It was as if she had forgotten basic motor functions. Meanwhile, Trevor scrambled backward, his eyes wide with terror.

"Stop!" Lucy screamed. But if Charlize heard her, it didn't register.

Finally, Charlize found purchase and rushed toward Trevor on all fours. The worms writhed about her abdomen, reaching out in different directions, sometimes latching onto nearby branches or rocks, only to be violently pulled away as Charlize bear-walked forward.

She pounced on Trevor like an animal. He put his arms up to catch her, which kept Charlize at bay; however, the stomach worms zeroed in on Trevor and began reaching for him.

He let out a scream as the first worm latched onto his jacket and began to burrow into the fabric.

"Fuck! Get her off me!" Trevor screamed. "Help!"

"Taste your fear... sweet. Succulent! Deliciousssssss," Charlize hissed.

Lucy rushed forward toward the pair. More of the worms had started to dig into Trevor's jacket just as she slammed into Charlize's body, knocking her to the side. Charlize crashed into a nearby boulder with a thump and let out a slight gasp of air. When she tried to get back up, Lucy kicked her head with the heel of her boot, bashing the woman's skull into the rock. It hit with a wet crack, and when she cocked her head to the side, blood flowed freely from an ugly gash.

Trevor tried to get up but couldn't find his footing. He tumbled back into the dirt and rocks. Lucy watched in horror as Charlize shifted her attention from Trevor to her.

"Your fear... it's deeper. Settled into your marrow. I just want to crack your bones open and slurp it down! Do you think they'll taste like men's bones?"

"Stop it," Lucy said, though it came out as a whisper.

Charlize let out a wet laugh. She got to her feet, then perched on top of the boulder as if she were a gargoyle.

"Do you hear that?" Charlize asked. She lifted a hand to her ear and acted as if she were listening to something. The worms gyrated in the same direction. "I can."

Lucy couldn't hear anything other than the beating of her own heart and her ragged breaths. But then...

...no...

...not now...

"Lucy?"

It was her brother's voice, coming from just behind a large pine tree.

Tears ran down Lucy's cheeks as she shook her head. "No, no, no... stop. Please!"

Charlize snapped her attention back to Lucy and smiled. It was a wide smile, wider than should have been possible.

"Why? Don't you want to see your brother? It has been oh so long. He became food for the worms," Charlize said. To accentuate her point, she ran her hand through the mass on her stomach as if it were a patch of hair. Some of the stringy things bit into her hand, only to get pulled away, leaving tiny bloody holes in her flesh as Charlize moved. "You left him all alone with Daddy, didn't you?"

Sobs came from all over. "Lucy, you left me. Didn't come back," her brother said.

Lucy took a shaky step back, trying to put distance between her and Charlize.

"Please," Lucy said, louder this time. "Make it stop."

A metallic click of a pistol's hammer cocking sounded in her ear. She could smell the gun oil, and it took her back to when she was twelve, watching her father clean his Smith & Wesson .38 revolver.

He'd given her a cold smile while she watched him clean. When he finished, he put one bullet in the cylinder, spun it, and then slammed it into place. Then he pointed it right at her.

"Let's see if it's your time you fairy faggot."

Lucy's father's voice boomed in her mind. He pulled the hammer back, producing the exact same metallic click. Then he squeezed the trigger.

A full body shiver ran through her just as something large crashed through the trees in the distance, pulling her out of the memory. Charlize peered in the direction of the sound and laughed, though it sounded more like a croak.

"It will be over soon. Food for the worms. Food for me," Charlize said.

Then she scurried off the rock on all fours. Lucy took another step back, but it was too late. Charlize lunged for her. Out of instinct, Lucy put her spear in front of her, catching Charlize in the torso. For half a second there was resistance before the point of the spear punched through clothing and then pierced skin.

Lucy watched in horror as Charlize grabbed the shaft of the spear with both hands. The worms wrapped around the wood as well. With agonizing effort, Charlize inched her way down the spear, impaling herself further but getting closer to Lucy.

"Soon, you'll all be nothing but memories for it. Experiences. Food," Charlize said through gritted teeth.

"Lucy, why did you leave me?" her brother asked.

Then came the boom of the pistol. It echoed through Lucy's mind, bouncing off the trees, sending birds to flight. She couldn't tell what was real anymore.

Lucy pushed Charlize to the side with the spear shaft and then let go before the worms could touch her. She knew if they got her, it would be the beginning of the end.

Charlize stumbled sideways, tripping over her own feet and hitting the ground. The spear's wooden shaft clanged on a rock as she fell, giving out a hollow thunk. However, it was only a moment before Charlize was back on her feet.

She looked down at the spear impaled in her chest. With a growl, Charlize grabbed onto the shaft and then hit it with her other hand, snapping the wood like it was nothing more than a twig. She flung the broken end away and turned toward Lucy, half the spear still sticking out of her back.

"Left me at the hands of that monster," Charlize said, though it wasn't her voice. It was Lucy's brother's voice coming out of her lips.

Charlize started to run, but an arrow struck her in the shoulder. Lucy glanced to the side and saw Trevor desperately trying to nock another arrow in his bow.

"And you! What a disappointment!" Charlize said, looking at Trevor. Though this time her voice shifted into a deeper pitch and tone, more like a man's.

Trevor stared at Charlize, not with horror, but with sadness. He finally nocked another arrow just as Charlize let out a guttural cry and rushed him. He let loose and the arrow hit Charlize in the eye. It burst out the backside of her skull with a loud crack and sent bits of blood, bone, and brain flying into the air.

Charlize toppled to the ground.

It took an eternity for Lucy to finally step toward Charlize's still-twitching body. She kept half-expecting Charlize to jump up and rush her like it was some sort of cheap horror movie jump scare. But none of that happened.

Charlize lay on her back staring at everything and nothing with her remaining eye. Trevor's arrow was still lodged in her other socket. Blood, bone, and bits of brain littered the dirt underneath her skull as well as something else. Something that made Lucy want to curl up into a ball and cry.

Worms. Thousands of tiny white worms wriggled throughout the gore as if it were some sort of macabre swimming pool.

Something touched Lucy's shoulder, and she spun around, screaming. Trevor was there, his eyes wide. He backed away with his hands up in the air.

"Sorry!" he said. "It's just me."

Lucy rushed over and threw her arms around him, craving nothing more than a warm embrace to make all this madness disappear. It only took him a moment to drop his bow and hug her back.

"What is happening?" Lucy asked.

"I don't know… I really don't know," he said.

Something rustling in the brush caught her attention. Trevor dropped to one knee and retrieved his bow, quickly nocking an arrow. Lucy grabbed her knife.

Hank pushed through the thick brush, his face covered with sweat and grime.

Lucy let out a sigh and put her knife away. Trevor muttered under his breath and put his arrow away.

"Where the fuck were you? We could have used your help," Lucy said.

Hank shot her a look of shame. "I'm no hero."

"That's fucking obvious," Trevor said.

"What? Is that supposed to make me feel bad or something? Heroes fucking die all the time, okay!"

Trevor took a few steps toward Hank, causing him to drop his pack and take a defensive stance.

"Will you two stop it, for fucks sake?" Lucy shouted.

That got both of their attention. Trevor looked at her and then back at Hank before throwing his hands in the air and backing off. Hank grumbled something under his breath and grabbed his gear.

"We're all going to die if we don't get off this fucking island. That's a fact. We have a better chance of making it if we work together. That's another fact. Otherwise…" Lucy let her words go unsaid and pointed at Charlize's body. "Now, let's get our shit together and get the fuck out of here."

As much as it pained her to leave Charlize unburied and out in the open like that, Lucy knew they didn't have much time before it was night. The sun was already on the descent, and it would be less than an hour before it was pitch dark out. That's when that *thing* would come around again. Besides, the less she had to be near those worms, the better. Just the thought of them made her skin crawl.

The three made their way toward the ruins. Lucy was lost in her own thoughts, unable to get her brother from her mind. There was nothing she could have done to save him. Or was there? Maybe if she had taken him with her...

All those thoughts were washed away when the ruins came into view. It was an old castle sitting on a small island in the middle of the crater lake. A ruined tower twisted up from the eastern side of the wall, though part of the roof and crenellations had long ago fallen away into the lake.

It was triangular in shape, with an open courtyard. The drawbridge... yes, it had a drawbridge, was down, allowing access to the castle. Moored to the dock was a small puddle jumper pontoon plane.

"Thank God," Hank said, wiping the sweat away from his face.

Lucy nodded in agreement. She glanced over to Trevor who stared at the building with a twisted expression on his face.

"You can fly that thing?" she asked.

He nodded. "Yeah, but I don't want to."

"We don't have a choice. The other option is to die here."

Trevor nodded again, but it didn't set Lucy's heart at ease.

Randall sat cross-legged on the ground facing the fireplace, the sacrificial dagger in front of him on the floor. Blood and bits of hair decorated the blade. The heat of the flames dried the blood that coated his arms and torso, making his skin sticky. The blood made the entire room smell of copper and metal, so thick Randall could taste it. He could taste the devotion in the blood. He could taste the fear underlying it all, and it was delicious.

The blood had belonged to one of the techs. One of the devoted. They had come to him, offering themselves to He Who Shall Devour the Stars, and Randall was more than happy to oblige. It was, in fact, part of the ritual, and the willing were much easier to work with than the unwilling.

The moment the dagger had pierced flesh and let the blood flow freely, there had been a distinct change in the air, like an electric charge that sensuously had tickled his body with the promise of power. It was but an appetizer for what was to come.

A small knock at the door broke him from his reverie.

"Enter," he said.

An intern walked in with a clipboard. She immediately covered her nose and mouth with her arm.

Disgust was close to fear. It didn't have as rich a taste, but Randall wasn't too picky these days.

"What is it?" he asked.

"Subject two was killed by the others," the woman said.

Randall smiled. "Excellent. It's all going as planned."

"They are closing in on the compound."

"He Who Shall Devour the Stars will feast on their marrow before the sunrise, and we will have a new chosen," Randall said. "Now leave me."

The intern turned and left the room. Once the door closed, Randall reached his hands into the body cavity of one of the other interns who lay dead in front of him. The blood was congealing, but still usable.

It was all going as planned.

Chapter Twenty-Eight

The trees opened into a small meadow maybe two hundred yards from the edge of the crater lake. Trevor stared in wonder at the size of the ruined castle. It was larger than he had anticipated. Being this close, he thought they could have been in Europe somewhere on a tour.

The old edifice stretched up nearly a hundred feet into the air at its highest point. For all intents and purposes, it looked abandoned. However, the sea plane moored to the dock said otherwise.

"You sure you can fly that?" Lucy asked.

Trevor nodded. He was familiar enough with planes that he would be able to get them into the air. Landing was another issue. He hadn't been as successful with that as he had with takeoffs.

"Let's get a bit closer and check it out," he said.

They moved slowly as they sneaked up toward the drawbridge. As they did, the red moss became more and more prevalent, covering the rocks and ground, and creeping up the trees. The trees afflicted with the stuff looked different—twisted somehow into a shadow of their former selves—and were oozing a black liquid from several lesions that covered their barky surfaces.

The moss itself was different as well, bolder than the few patches they had come across out in the wilderness. The stuff was everywhere, covering entire swaths of ground like a crimson blanket. What more, the flowers were blooming, flesh-like in color and appearance and pulsating with something akin to a heartbeat.

Trevor walked over to a nearby fallen pine that was covered in the corpulent blooms. A chill ran up his spine as the flowers slowly turned toward him as one and began to undulate closer to him. Thin, almost translucent feelers, too reminiscent of tapeworms, wriggled out from the petals of the nearest flower, reaching out toward him, writhing, and whipping about.

More and more of the wormy strands appeared across the tree, all reaching for him. It was horrifying and somewhat mesmerizing the way they whipped and whorled around in a frenzy. Trevor couldn't help but imagine what it would be like to be one of them. One with them.

He reached his hand out toward the feelers. The hair on his arm stood at end as the wispy tendrils stretched even further trying to grasp onto his fingertips.

Someone jerked him backward by the hood of his jacket. He hit the ground, wincing as his ass cheek slammed into a jutted rock.

"Wha..." he tried to form words, but they refused to come together.

Trevor looked around and found Lucy standing over him. She was talking, saying something, but he couldn't hear her. In fact, he couldn't hear anything, just a low droning in the back of his mind.

Lucy crouched down next to him, grabbed him by the chin, and looked deep into one eye, then the next. She spoke again, and this time he could hear her voice, though it was muffled, like she was trying to talk to him through a wall or pillow.

Trevor shook his head, rubbing at his temples.

"...can you hear me?" Lucy asked. She whispered, but her voice was sharp, cutting through the din.

Trevor still couldn't speak, but he nodded.

"Good. What the fuck? What the hell were you doing?" Lucy asked.

"I..." He thought about it for a moment. Why had he been so close to the flowers? "I don't know. It was like something came over me. I *needed* to touch them."

Lucy gave him a hard look then stood. "New rule. We stay away from the strange worm flowers, got it?"

She didn't require an answer and instead helped Trevor back to his feet.

"Good rule," Trevor said.

Hank nodded, and they continued to make their way closer to the castle, which appeared abandoned, save for the plane docked out front. From a decent vantage point that provided good cover, they watched. After a few minutes, a man toting a shotgun appeared in the doorway, stepped outside, and lit a cigarette.

Trevor recognized the man from before. It was the same muscle-bound guard wearing a tactical uniform that had been posted outside the compound when he first landed on the other island. He shifted his focus from the guard to the plane. Now that he was closer, he recognized the make and shook his head.

"What is it?" Lucy asked.

"This kind of plane requires a key to start. What do you want to bet they didn't leave it hanging in the ignition."

"Well, that's fucking great," Hank said, crossing his arms across his chest. "Fucking our luck, yeah?"

"That just means we'll have to verify if the keys are in there, and if not, get the keys. The plan is still the same—get the hell out of here. Right?" Lucy said, staring at the guard.

"I guess, but how the hell are we going to check the plane for keys with the goon squad out front?"

Trevor motioned to the armed guard out front. Lucy placed her hand on Trevor's shoulder.

"I'll take care of him. Wait here exactly five minutes, then distract the guard."

Trevor's mind raced at the possibilities of what was about to happen. "Distract him? How? Should I go out there and sing him a song?"

Lucy smiled. "Whatever it takes. Five minutes."

With that, Lucy padded back into the forest and out of sight. Trevor tried to ask her more questions but either she didn't hear him, or she ignored him. Either way, she was gone now. He cast an incredulous look to Hank and mouthed, *what the fuck?* Hank shrugged.

Trevor checked his watch, marked the time, and leaned against the deadfall. He massaged his buttocks, which were still sore from falling on the rock, and wondered how the hell he was going to distract the very disgruntled looking gentleman with a shotgun.

Perhaps he could do a little Irish jig out in the open? Or maybe make some crazy animal sounds. Something told him that would likely get him shot more than anything.

"Tyler needs the operation," Hank said.

Trevor looked over at his shoulder to Hank and found him sitting on the ground with his legs outstretched. He was mumbling something under his breath, his face scrunched up like he was in a heated argument with somebody.

"What?" Trevor whispered.

Hank looked up at him with bloodshot eyes.

"Emmett promised he would help us out. I mean, look, we're not poor, but we can't afford that kind of money, and the insurance says they won't cover even a quarter of it. Something about a preexisting condition. How the fuck can they say something like that?"

Hank's voice rose in volume. Trevor looked at the guard hoping he hadn't heard them. Thankfully, the man was still leaning against the wall of the old castle, oblivious to their presence.

Trevor put a finger to his lips and shushed Hank.

"You have to be quiet," he said.

"Of course, it was a preexisting condition. He was fucking born with a bad heart! It doesn't get any more preexisting than that!"

Trevor checked his watch. They still had two minutes before he was supposed to distract the guard. If Hank didn't lower his voice though, they were going to fulfill their end of the bargain early.

Trevor duck-walked over to Hank, keeping a low profile, and put a hand on the man's shoulder. "What are you talking about?"

"My son. He needs a heart transplant otherwise he'll die young. We're on the waiting list, but the fucking insurance agents are doing everything in their power to ensure we don't get any help. Fucking sharks.

"I mean, Emmett said he would help, and they have the money, but this was his fucking idea. Come out on this show with me. It will double the chances of one of us winning if we both go. I mean, fish in a barrel, right? We both know our way around a camp, and yeah, if we won, that would be it, baby. But... something changed in Emmett. He wasn't himself."

Trevor sat there, unsure of what to say or do. This was the most Hank had spoken for some time, and now he was pouring his heart out to him.

"Look, I'm sorry about your son, I really am. But if we don't get off this island, then nobody is going to be there to help your kid, right? So, let's focus and get the hell out of Dodge, okay?"

Hank stared at Trevor for a moment then started mumbling again. Trevor shook his head and looked at the watch.

It was time.

Out of time and out of options, Trevor followed his gut. He stood and walked out into the open toward the guard.

It only took the man a second to see him. He flipped his cigarette down and raised the shotgun.

"Stop right there!"

Trevor raised his hands in the air. "Look, I don't want to be any trouble, but my friend is really hurt. We need a medevac out of this place to a hospital!"

The guard kept the shotgun trained on Trevor but started moving forward. There was something predatory in the way he moved, and Trevor would have bet money he was ex-military or had received some sort of special training.

"On your knees, now!"

Trevor complied. He tried to see if Lucy was anywhere to be found, but she was nowhere in sight. He cursed himself for being so foolish.

The guard stopped about two feet away from Trevor, the barrel of the shotgun pointed directly at his face.

"How many of you are there?"

"Just me and my friend," Trevor said, nodding back toward the bushes. The guard glanced over in the same direction, and Trevor caught movement from behind the man.

Lucy rushed up from behind and hit him with a rock.

Chapter Twenty-Nine

The guard dropped to his knees, trying to turn toward Lucy but falling instead onto the ground in a heap. Lucy's hands shook as the realization of what she had just done hit her. She glanced at the rock in her hand covered with blood and bits of hair. Would it taste like metal? Or would it taste delicious?

Lucy shook her head and dropped it to the ground. When she looked back at the guard, it was not the man at all but her brother's small frame.

The image was only in her mind for a split-second, but it was more than enough to rattle her.

"No… I…" The words were lost in her throat, covered by a deep sob that rumbled from her core. She fell to her knees next to the fallen guard and placed a hand on his leg.

Again, she had killed another human being. Lucy couldn't deny it anymore. She was a killer. It was in her blood.

The guard moved, ever so slightly, and a wave of relief flowed through Lucy. He was alive! Perhaps she wasn't a killer at all.

Self-preservation took over, and Lucy grabbed the guard's shotgun before he could regain his senses. She struggled back to her feet and wiped her face, hopefully clearing the tears but sure that she just smeared dirt and grime around.

The guard let out another pained groan. Lucy kicked him in the leg. "Where are the keys to the plane?"

He moaned but didn't answer. Trevor ran up next to Lucy and placed a hand on her shoulder.

"You okay?"

"No, I'm not fucking okay." Lucy kicked the guard again, harder this time. "Where are the keys? We want off this damn island!"

The guard let out a pained sound as he got to his hands and knees. Lucy kept the shotgun trained on him, halfway expecting him to lash out with a knife, or throw dirt in her eyes like this was some sort of crappy action movie fight. Instead, he shuddered and fell to the ground again.

She let out a frustrated sigh and looked over at Trevor. He nodded, apparently reading her mind as he crept over to the side of the guard and used his foot to roll him over. Lucy immediately wished he hadn't done so.

The guard screamed in pain as he rolled onto his back. Nearly a dozen long, stringy worms had attached to his face from the red moss on the ground, pulling like bungee cords until finally popping away from the ground and from his face.

Scarlet irritation and rashes ringed out from where each of the worms had burrowed into his exposed skin. Lucy sucked in a deep breath and took a step back, Trevor following suit.

The guard's eyes were open wide, and he brought a shaky hand up to his face, grabbing one of the exposed worms. It was already trying to dig deeper into his cheek. He screamed as he started pulling it out, and Lucy watched in horror as he pulled at least six inches of bloody worm out of his cheek.

The guard lost his grip on the wriggling creature, and it immediately started to burrow back in. He screamed and grabbed at it again, but this time when he pulled, a bloody flap of skin and meat came loose. He sat there staring at the piece of himself in between his dirty, bloody, fingers and then looked at Lucy with eyes full of rage, pain, and something else.

Hunger.

The guard grabbed at his face with both hands, and more and more of his skin came away in gory patches. His screaming got louder as he began to convulse. Frothy blood bubbled up from his lips, and he arched his back.

"Do something," Trevor said.

Lucy heard the words, but it was background noise, not unlike the ringing of tinnitus or a television playing in the other room. On one level, she registered what he said and agreed wholeheartedly that she should do something. On another, her body didn't know what to do and refused to move.

The guard opened and closed his mouth as if he were a fish out of water. Each time more and more blood poured out. With the blood came more worms—wriggling and writhing in the ruby pool.

Lucy swore she could hear the worms screaming with ecstasy as they lapped up the liquid and devoured the guard's flesh and muscle.

"Lucy!"

Was it Trevor? It sounded more like her brother.

The guard's eye bulged, and he turned his head to look directly at her. He let out a soft mewling noise as a bundle of the worms pushed their way free from behind his socket, popping the eye out. It dangled there, hanging from his face attached only by a meaty string of nerves and blood vessels.

Then the guard stopped moving and fell backward onto the ground once again. He shook and twitched a few more times before laying still.

Lucy let out a deep breath she had been holding and relaxed her shoulders before casting a glance at Trevor. He stood next to her, eyes wide, and pale as snow.

"What the fuck?" Trevor said through heavy breathing. "What in the actual fuck?!"

Lucy was about to answer but the guard sat upright and hacked up a wad of worms onto the ground. Then he turned toward her and started to pull himself up from the dirt.

"S-soooooo, hungry…" the guard said.

"Don't move!" Lucy said, pointing the shotgun at him.

The guard glanced at her with his remaining eye and licked his lips, which only spread the blood around more. Then he cast a hungry smile at her. "You'll do."

He moved faster than Lucy thought possible. The guard sprang to his feet and took two steps before Lucy yanked the trigger on the shotgun more out of instinct than anything else. The weapon barked, slamming into her shoulder as she hadn't properly set the butt of the shotgun against it. If it had been a rifle, she might have missed, but it's difficult to miss a target at close range with a shotgun.

The blast hit high and right but obliterated the guard's arm. He stumbled and groaned with pain but continued to move forward, only a couple of feet from Lucy.

Lucy pumped another shell into the chamber and squeezed the trigger, careful to hold the weapon properly this time.

It barked again, and this time caught the guard center mass, dropping him onto the ground right in front of Lucy.

With her ears ringing and the taste and smell of gunpowder heavy in the air, Lucy racked another shell into the chamber. She was about to shoot again when Trevor put a hand on her arm, pushing the barrel of the shotgun away from the guard.

"He's dead," Trevor said and nodded at the body.

There was a bloody patch on the back of his shirt with dozens of tiny holes where the shot had passed through the guard's chest.

They both stood in silence for some time. Lucy kept the weapon aimed at the guard's body, but it didn't move again. It wasn't long before the worms began to feast on his wounds. She finally used her boot to roll him over and looked away when she saw his face was covered in a wriggling mass.

The guard had a pistol that Trevor took. A quick search of the man's pockets, careful not to touch any of the worms, revealed no keys to the plane. Another search of the plane brought a similar outcome.

"They must be inside the castle somewhere," Trevor said.

"Then let's go get them. Where the fuck is Hank?"

At the mention of his name, Hank came out onto the road and gave them a sheepish grin. "Here."

"I'm starting to notice a pattern with you!" Lucy said.

Hank shrugged. "Looked like you had it handled."

Lucy didn't have the energy to argue, so she just nodded. "Let's go."

Trevor shook his head and handed the pistol to Hank. "Maybe you can do something with this."

Hank took the gun, popped the magazine out, and ensured there were bullets before slamming it back into the magazine well and racking the slide.

The castle itself was in worse shape than Lucy had thought now that they were closer. Part of the wall had fallen or crumbled away, leaving piles of stone bricks piled near the base. More of that red moss had begun to collect in the cracks and seams between bricks, giving the impression that the castle itself was bleeding. She was eager to get off the island, even more so now, and if she never saw moss again, it would be too soon.

The trio approached the big wooden doorway, reinforced with blackened steel hinges. It was a modern door but made to look rustic and from the era. Lucy knew it was very sturdy even without touching it. She prayed it wasn't locked because they didn't have the time or energy to bust it down.

Her prayers were answered, and the door opened easily. An entryway stood in front of them, with a hallway of stone and rotted wood leading to T-junction about twenty yards down.

There was a metal stool just inside the doorway with a coat rack next to it. Sitting on top of the chair was one of the envelopes. This time it had Hank's name on it. Trevor picked it up and handed it over.

Hank tucked the pistol into his waistband and opened it up. Lucy watched Hank as he read through the letter. She didn't like the expression he had or the way he furrowed his brow, looking up at Lucy from time to time.

"What's it say?" Trevor asked.

Hank dropped the envelope. It flitted through the air before landing on the ground at his feet. He shook his head, rubbing at his temples and mumbling under his breath. It was hard to hear what he was saying, but it was something about his kid and needing the money.

"Hank?" Lucy said, taking a step closer.

Hank growled and pulled the gun from his waistband and pointed it at Lucy. Tears were just starting to form in the corners of his eyes.

"I'm sorry," he said. "I have to."

Chapter Thirty

Trevor ran toward Hank as he lifted the pistol, hoping to close the distance and tackle him to the ground. Hank must have caught the movement out of the corner of his eye and turned the gun on Trevor.

Trevor didn't register the noise of the shot other than a dull pop. Yet the sensation of something slamming into his shoulder put him off balance, and he crashed to the ground. It was only a few moments later when the pain blossomed in his arm.

He gritted his teeth and sucked in some air. Hank took a step closer and pointed the gun at his face.

"I'm so sorry. I don't want to do this," Hank said.

Tears streamed down his face, and he bit his lower lip. Trevor knew this was the end for him. Hank was going to shoot him in head, and that would be it. No restarts. No extra lives. Game over, man. Game over.

Trevor thought about begging for his life, but there was a small voice in the back of his head that told him to accept what was coming and embrace the darkness of the void.

So, he closed his eyes and waited for the release.

There came a blast, causing Trevor to suck in a deep breath as he waited for it to all be over.

Trevor wondered if this was what it was like to be dead. No more hurting.

But there was pain. His shoulder still hurt. On some level, he could tell he was still starved and dehydrated. Wasn't there supposed to be a bright light?

He opened an eye and looked around. Hank sat slumped against the wall, looking down at his chest. His coat was ripped up and bloody, and the wall behind him was streaked with it as well. Hank looked over at Trevor and then past him.

Trevor rolled to his side to get a better vantage, and found Lucy standing there, smoke wafting from the barrel of the shotgun.

She had a determined look chiseled into her face and appeared to be on the verge of tears. Trevor got up, gasping as a jolt of white-hot pain burst in his wounded shoulder.

"Fuck," he said through gritted teeth.

Hank watched him from the ground, opened his mouth like he was about to say something, then slumped over.

"Holy shit, that was close," Trevor said. He glanced at Lucy, who still held the shotgun pointed at Hank's lifeless body. "Hey, you okay?"

Lucy didn't respond. She kept whispering something about her brother.

"Lucy?" He walked over, but something grated in his shoulder. It felt like bone on bone, which wasn't good at all. He yelled and dropped to the ground.

That got Lucy's attention. She came over to his side but still had that faraway look in her eyes. When she looked at him and his bloody shoulder, Lucy put the gun down and opened Trevor's coat to get a better look.

It hurt to move, and the fact that Lucy jostled him around didn't help at all. He hissed when she peeled the coat and his shirt away to reveal the bare skin beneath.

"How is it?" he asked.

Lucy shook her head then rolled him to his side. More pain erupted when she pulled the shirt from the backside, as it had stuck to his skin due to the blood.

"Looks like it went through. But you'll need to see a doctor soon. We need to try and stop the bleeding."

Trevor nodded as Lucy took her coat off. After that, she ripped a big chunk of her undershirt up, creating a few makeshift bandages.

"We really need to clean this, but I guess we'll have to make do with what we have," Lucy said.

"What? Dirty bandages aren't good enough?"

Lucy looked up, and Trevor shot her a wink and his best smile despite the pain. She returned the smile and then got back to work.

"So, you're making jokes even though you just got shot in the shoulder, eh?"

"Well, it's either that or cry, I guess," Trevor said as tears ran down his face. "Or both."

Lucy pressed the first of the bandages onto the gunshot after cleaning it as best she could with the water she had left. Trevor groaned as she applied the pressure and fought to keep his bile down. This was a pain he wasn't used to, and it hurt like a sonofabitch.

"You might still cry," Lucy said as she finished tying off the bandage on his shoulder. "It isn't perfect, and you still need to see a doctor ASAP, but at least this should help a little."

"Thanks," Trevor said. "It's the best we got, and better than I could have managed by myself."

Lucy got up and staggered over to Hank's body. She kicked him in the thigh, and then, apparently happy there was no response, she crouched down next to him. After digging through his coat, she pulled out choice items like a knife, his canteen, and fire-making materials.

Trevor sat against the wall, taking a moment to try to focus on his breathing. Every time he moved, his shoulder reminded him that it had a huge hole through it.

"What the...?" Lucy said.

"What is it?"

"Look at this!"

Trevor looked over to where Lucy was crouched down. She had her back to him and was slowly crab-walking backward with the letter from the envelope in her hand.

"What?"

She waved him over with the letter, still staring at the wall behind Hank's body. Trevor started to get up, let out a pained hiss as he stood, and then wobbled over to Lucy.

"What is it?" he said again as he got closer.

Lucy pointed to the blood-stained wall with the letter.

Trevor looked over. At first, it seemed like it was simply blood with bits of cloth and meaty giblets. However, a cold pit formed in his stomach as he watched the meaty bits wriggle and move.

It wasn't just blood and giblets. There were worms.

Hundreds of them, chewing, gnashing, and tearing the tiny meaty bits that clung to the stonework. Trevor wondered if they were in him now. He could almost feel them feeding on him from the inside out. Or perhaps it was just his mind playing tricks—or blood loss. Perhaps it was the hunger that had settled deep in his marrow where the darkness lived.

Trevor backed away, stumbled over a loose rock, and tumbled to the ground. The bile he'd been fighting to keep at bay clawed its way up his throat and found a new home next to Hank's boot. Trevor was at least happy to see there were no worms in his vomit.

Lucy came over and helped him back up.

"You okay?"

Trevor shook his head. "Not really, but I'll live. For now, anyway."

Lucy handed him the letter. "Look at that," she said.

Trevor grabbed the letter, and his heart sank with the words that were elaborately printed upon the cardstock.

Kill Lucy and Trevor. $1,000,000.

"What the fuck?" Trevor said under his breath.

"It's getting real," Lucy said.

"Real shitty."

Hank's foot twitched.

Trevor and Lucy backed away. Lucy scrambled over to the shotgun and pumped another shell into the chamber.

"Hank?" Trevor said.

Hank's body began to spasm. Frothy blood bubbled up from his lips and his chest wound, along with more of the alabaster worms.

"Let's go," Lucy said, tugging at Trevor's coat.

"Yeah."

They both backed away, further into the castle, but before they could exit the entryway, Hank sat up. He sniffed the air for a moment before snapping his head toward Lucy and Trevor.

"I can smell you," Hank said. However, his voice wasn't his. It was deeper, full of phlegm and gravel. "And you smell delicious!"

"I'll blow your fucking head off," Lucy said as she aimed the shotgun at him.

He laughed at that and then stood. Hank swayed as if there was a strong wind and caught himself on the wall with an outstretched hand. His laughter became deeper until it sounded more like a whooping bark from a hyena.

His fingers popped, and elongated, peeling skin as talons punched through.

"This isn't happening," Trevor whispered.

The shotgun roared as it spat fire. Trevor flinched but couldn't peel his eyes away as the shot slammed into Hank's body again. Hank let out a grunt, but looked at them with red, bloodshot eyes and grinned.

"Dinnertime," he said.

With that, he sprinted toward them. Lucy and Trevor turned and ran deeper into the castle with Hank gaining on them.

The castle beyond the entrance was dark with only a few torches providing a meager light. The red moss covered the walls, making it hot and muggy inside. Trevor did his best to keep away from the moss, knowing full well what would happen if he let it touch him.

They turned a corner and found a doorway. Lucy grabbed Trevor with one hand and pulled him inside. There was a rickety wooden door, not much, but something was better than nothing, and Lucy closed it quickly but softly.

Not two seconds later, Hank's heavy boots sounded in the hallway right outside of the door. Trevor let out a sigh of relief when they continued to pound further away.

That relief was short-lived when an awful stench of rotten meat and mildew hit his nose. Trevor turned to find the floor of the room covered in bones. Bones from deer, elk, moose, and even bear. Bones from humans.

They were in something's den.

That's when Trevor found Burke's headless body, partially devoured and stuffed in the corner.

"Jesus..." he said.

Lucy sucked in her breath and grabbed him by the unhurt shoulder. "We need to get out of here."

A low growl caused Trevor's heart to skip a beat. The clack of bones shifting caught his attention, and he looked over at the source. At first, he thought it was just another dead elk, but the skull was too big and somewhat misshapen. Then it moved.

Lavender eyes glowed to life from within the skull and it stood on two legs. In the gloom, it was hard to see, but it was taller than a human by more than half. It was the creature. It was Him.

The thing looked right at Trevor and roared.

Chapter Thirty-One

When the creature roared, Lucy fired the shotgun out of pure instinct. The shot slammed into the thing's thigh, taking a bloody chunk from its leg.

The creature howled in pain, and as it did, the moss, which was covering almost the entire surface of the room, lit up with a deep ruby color. It seemed to pulse with the same intensity as the monster's wail.

Fleshy flowers bloomed on the moss, bigger than what Lucy had seen before. They started to glow with the same lavender color as the creature's eyes, undulating in a strange dance that was both mesmerizing and sickening.

Even with the wound, the creature bounded toward her quicker than she could follow. It swiped the shotgun from her hand and shoulder-checked her into the wall. She slammed into the moss-covered stone and saw stars as the air blasted from her lungs.

Trevor pulled the pistol with his good arm and started shooting. One of the bullets tore into the thing's shoulder and whipped its attention toward him. Trevor continued to fire, but the thing was too fast, running across the floor and then up the wall like it was a squirrel climbing up a tree. His shots slapped into the moss with wet thuds, sending bits of the stuff flying into the air.

Lucy rolled to her side, her lungs refusing to work. Each movement was a monumental struggle, with her brain going on strike as her body struggled for oxygen.

Lucy put her hand down on the ground and didn't notice the big patch of moss before it was too late. As soon as her bare skin touched it, tendrils of the stuff burrowed into her skin. The fleshy flower petals, acting like a Venus flytrap on steroids, bit into her forearms. Dozens of the glowing worms wriggled out from the folds of the moss and started devouring her flesh.

Lucy tried to scream, but she still couldn't breathe, and only a gasping wheeze came out.

The pain was intense, almost blinding, but there was something else there, just below the surface of it all. It was like a cloying ecstasy in the pain. The promise of something different if she just let herself go.

Lucy fought against the feeling with everything she could muster. A big part of her wanted to give in though, let the darkness take her and the worms tear the flesh and muscle from her body before devouring the marrow in her bones.

There was a kind of peace in knowing that if she stopped fighting, it could all be over. All the pain. All of the suffering. She could float in oblivion and no longer feel anything.

"Lucy."

The voice was faint, but it snapped her attention back to the grueling reality of worms burrowing into her body.

It was her brother.

The background noise of the den faded away, replaced with the sound of an off-balanced ceiling fan whooping above her. Alanis Morisette's "Hand in My Pocket" played on a cheap CD player sitting on the edge of a beat-up dresser.

It was dark, but Lucy knew this place. It would forever be scarred into her memory, unwilling to let go. Perhaps if Lucy let the worms feed on her body, she could finally find peace.

Lucy looked all around her, but the worms were gone. It was just her room, right down to the hole in the drywall her father had gifted her with. Then, a moment later, the song stopped suddenly. The room went dark. Lucy could navigate her house blindfolded if she had to, so even though it had been years, she was still able to pad over to her nightstand and flick the lamp on.

It was still her room, but everything was cleaned up, put away, and covered in old sheets. It's how her mother made it up when she left.

Her brother, Jeff, cried from his room. The walls were thin in the old house, and you could hear a mouse fart at night if you listened close enough.

Lucy walked over to the wall that separated their rooms and placed her hand against it.

"Jeff?"

"Why did you leave me? Why didn't you take me with you!?"

"I couldn't, I—"

A gunshot rang out in Jeff's room as a bullet ripped through the drywall right next to Lucy's face. She ran to the hallway and toward his bedroom. Lucy already knew what she would find—her brother, dead on the floor, gun in hand, blood everywhere, glistening in the moonlight that spilled in through his window. Yet, nothing could have prepared her for what she saw.

As she opened the door, her words caught in her throat. Jeff's body sagged against the wall, just like she thought he would be. Brain, bone, and blood painted the wall just behind him like always. But instead of gunshot wounds, foot-long worms pulsating in that same violet hue were wriggling into the entry wound on his face.

He turned toward her and gave Lucy a meek smile. His eyes glowed with the same energy as the worms. All around them, the bedroom began to pulse with the light in sync with the worms.

"I can finally see," he said.

His voice was distant and overwhelmingly close at the same time. She heard the voices of their mother and father along with Jeff's. There were so many voices speaking, screaming, crying, and laughing all at the same time, yet, somehow, Jeff's was the loudest.

"See what?"

There was pain just below her eye, like someone had an ice pick and was slowly driving it into her sinus cavity. Yet, it was dull, almost an afterthought.

Jeff turned toward her more, and one of the worms crawled into his ear. "I can see Him and He is glorious."

Jeff's eyes stopped pulsating and instead glowed with a violet intensity that was blinding. Lucy screamed, but the laughter of a thousand voices drowned out her cries.

Randall's body buzzed with power. It was an energy he hadn't felt in a very long time, and it was intoxicating. Like a high to beat all other highs. Euphoric.

He walked over to the mirror on the wall and pulled his robe off, letting it fall to the floor in a clump of silk. Randall gazed at his form in the mirror and smiled.

Thousands of tiny, violet-hued, worms wriggled just beneath his skin. Gunshots popped in the next room over, but he paid them no mind. They were no threat to him. The time drew nigh...

Chapter Thirty-Two

Trevor's muscles refused his command to run, fight, or do anything at all. But the monstrosity before him was too much for his mind to handle. The thing stood taller than any animal he'd ever encountered. It had to be more than fifteen feet, and that wasn't counting the rack of elk-like antlers protruding from its head.

At first glance, it looked like it was maybe an elk or deer skull, but the shape was off. Its brow and eye sockets were more human-like, and the teeth! Rows of sharp teeth sprouted from its jaw like jagged glass.

Dark fur covered the creature's spindly body, but as Trevor stared, he saw it wasn't fur at all. It was millions of worms.

The thing picked Lucy from the ground, and she began to scream. Her scream was cut off as her eyes began to glow violet like the creature's. It opened its mouth wide, and a sick crack echoed through the room as it unhinged its jaws as if it were a snake.

It was going to eat Lucy.

Trevor pointed the pistol at the creature and took aim. It was risky since the thing had Lucy in its hands, but if he didn't do something quickly, it wouldn't matter. It was already bringing her limp body towards its mouth.

Trevor pulled the trigger over and over again until the pistol emptied. Some of the shots missed, going wide or too high, but once the first bullet ripped into the creature's wormy flesh, he sent the rest into the same area.

The thing roared with pain, dropping Lucy to the ground. Its glowing eyes narrowed in on him. The bullets had hurt the thing, but it was obvious it was far from death.

The creature dropped to all fours and sprinted right at him. Trevor jumped out of the way at the last moment, hitting the ground hard and grunting in pain as a jagged piece of bone pierced his thigh. He expected the thing to be on him any second, but to his surprise, it rushed out of the room and out of sight.

Trevor rolled over and looked at Lucy. She lay crumpled on the ground amongst the bones and detritus.

"Lucy? You alive?" Trevor asked.

She didn't answer. He crawled over to Lucy and rolled her onto her back, careful to cradle her head. Lucy's eyes were open, no longer glowing with the violet energy but also staring at nothing. She was still breathing though, which Trevor took as a good sign.

"Hey, you okay?" he asked. "Lucy?"

Still, she didn't answer. Trevor dragged her over to a part of the floor that wasn't covered in the moss or worms and tried to make her as comfortable as possible.

"I'm going to go find the keys to the plane and get us out of here. Stay put."

Trevor had no idea if she could hear him, but he did know that they needed to get out of the castle as soon as possible. He hoped that thing wouldn't come back while he was out, but dragging Lucy's body around while trying to find the keys wasn't an option. Trevor needed to conserve what little energy he had left to drag her back to the plane and avoid Hank.

Trevor found the shotgun on the ground nearby and picked it up. He conducted a quick check and found it only had three shells left. Better than nothing, but not enough to give him a lot of comfort. With a final glance at Lucy, he crept out of the room and made his way down the hall.

Somehow, the hallway was even stuffier than the creature's den. Maybe it was lack of airflow or perhaps something else, but the walls pressed down on Trevor, and an uneasy sense of claustrophobia settled into his guts.

The shotgun was a small comfort, but after watching that thing get shot without much effect, the gun didn't seem as useful. But a weird man-eating monster wasn't the only danger in this place. There were still the guards—and Hank.

Trevor turned the corner to find a doorway kicked in from the outside. The door hung at an odd angle, its jamb splintered. Inside was what appeared to be a breakroom with a medium-sized folding table, a cooler in the corner, a couple of camp lanterns, and an array of dead guards on the floor.

With a trembling hand, Trevor kept the shotgun pointed at them, halfway expecting them to jump up at any moment and charge him like cannibalistic zombies. However, the amount of blood on the floor and the lack of movement from the three security professionals told him they were probably done for.

One guard, a short but muscular man with a pointed goatee, had his throat ripped out. The coppery scent of it was almost overpowering and made Trevor want to throw up. The other two were face down, but one of their arms was snapped and was positioned at an angle that wasn't natural in any stretch of the imagination.

"I can smell you. The scent of your fear is delicious."

It was Hank.

Trevor snapped the shotgun toward the back of the room. The lanterns were on but didn't shed a ton of light, so it was hard to see.

"Hank? Let's talk about this. You need some help, buddy."

A wet laugh emanated from the shadows.

"I don't think so. Never felt better, *buddy.*"

The darkness shifted and out stepped Hank. Or at least, what Trevor thought might have once been Hank. The man walked with a strange gait, strides longer than normal and his back somewhat hunched over. Blood covered almost every inch of him.

When he stepped into the light, Trevor sucked in a sharp breath. It wasn't blood. Thousands of worms wriggled all across his body.

The wriggling parasites all moved toward Trevor, as if they were trying to pull Hank closer to his prey. The worms weren't the worst part. Hank's eyes were gone, leaving gaping pits that seeped with a brackish ooze. Not only that, but small antlers had burst through the skin on Hank's forehead, creating bloody little nubs of bone that glistened in the lantern's light.

Moving more like an animal than a man, Hank crouched down and sniffed the air. The security guard nearest to him let out a slight groan of pain and started to push himself up on his hands and knees.

Hank crawled over to the man quicker than should have been possible. He pounced onto the man's back and grabbed him by the chin. The guard let out a guttural cry and fell back to the floor.

Trevor was frozen. He wanted to run but couldn't look away as Hank pulled. The guard's cry turned from fear into pain as his neck first stretched then tore. Blood spewed from several rips and then came a sickening crack and tear as Hank pulled the pulled the man's head off.

"I'm going to enjoy eating your insides," Hank said as he reached down and ripped a piece of flesh off the dead man's head.

Trevor's mind raced. He still needed to find the keys to the plane, but Hank was a wildcard, and that thing was still in the castle somewhere. Running wasn't an option anymore. He was too tired, and Hank and that monster were faster.

In the back of the room was a closed door. This one was metal, and if it were unlocked, then maybe Trevor could get into it and secure it from the other side. It might buy him some time.

"You know, you should just let me eat you. Sure, you'll be dead, but for that moment where your soul is still attached to your flesh bag, when the worms burrow into your brain, it will be wild. Trust me."

As he tried to move as quietly as possible toward the door, Trevor did his best to ignore Hank. Hank continued to babble on about the worms and devouring him, but Trevor took it one step at a time, choosing his foot placement as if he were stalking a deer.

Hank didn't seem to hear him as he continued to devour chunks of the guard's neck and head and talk to the front of the room where Trevor had been. After a grueling dozen steps, Trevor finally made it to the metal doorway.

He reached out and grabbed the handle, pressed the latch, and pulled. It was locked, and it let out a slight noise as it shifted.

Hank's head snapped toward Trevor, and a bloody smile appeared on his face.

"There you are," Hank said.

Chapter Thirty-Three

Lucy opened her eyes. She was on her back staring up at the ceiling of her brother's bedroom. The light was off, making it hard to see, but the moonlight provided a little illumination. The room stunk of blood mixed with shit, body odor, and the metallic, smoky scent of a gunshot.

It was all at once familiar and terrifying. It didn't help that everything in her body hurt like she had fallen from a roof or rolled down a mountainside. Lucy coughed and the coppery taste of blood filled her mouth. When she wiped her mouth, her hand came away with light streaks of red. Lucy reached up with her other hand but stopped short of her face. A strange pain formed in her forearm. For a few moments, she simply stared at her arm, trying to figure out what was up. It didn't feel broken. She'd broken her shin when she was twenty after tripping on deadfall in some mountains near Denver.

This was different. It was deep, but it wasn't bone. There wasn't any damage to her coat, no heavy blood stains or anything like that. She started to roll her sleeve up, the pain intensified, and she let out a soft yelp followed by a sharp intake of breath.

As gently as possible, she rolled the sleeve up, exposing her forearm. At first, she couldn't see anything, and then it moved.

One of those damned worms was burrowing into her flesh. Its body pulsed and wriggled as it crawled a little deeper into her arm. Now that she could see it, it somehow hurt even more. The thought of one of those things inside of her made Lucy want to throw up and cry. It was eating her from the inside.

Fighting back a scream, Lucy pulled her knife out and prodded the end of the worm. It writhed at the cold steel's touch, causing a spasm of agony to flare all the way up her shoulder. Lucy looked all around her and finally found a small stick. She grabbed it and shoved it in her mouth before grabbing the end of the worm with her hand.

That sent it wriggling even harder, and it was all she could do to keep a grip on the thing as it struggled to get away from her touch and completely into her body. The thing was hot to the touch and almost soggy.

Lucy bit down hard and pulled on it. It didn't want to budge, and she was afraid it might tear in half. That thought didn't sit well with her. Would the other half burrow into her body? After another tug, it unlatched. It was an odd sensation, and the feeling of it sliding out from her arm was nauseating. Lucy made slight mewing sounds as the worm seemed endless. She had already pulled nearly six inches of the thing out of her arm. Finally, it popped out.

Almost immediately, it searched for another purchase on her skin. Lucy screamed, the stick falling away, as she flung the worm far from her.

The tears refused to stay bottled up and flowed freely down her face. Lucy clutched her knees to her chest, wishing that it was all a dream and that she wasn't back home in her brother's room, his lifeless corpse smiling at her. Or...

The sounds of her old home ceased in an instant, leaving her in silence. Lucy looked around. Instead of Jeff's bedroom, she was in a room full of bones. She was in the den.

Reality slammed back into her like a sledgehammer. Perhaps it was something in the worm, a toxic bite, or hallucinogenic substance. Or maybe she was just exhausted, malnourished, and dehydrated. Either way, she needed to get out of here.

"Trevor?"

Her voice was raw, and it hurt to talk. Nobody was in the room with her. At least that thing wasn't there anymore. Its violet eyes boring through her mind. She would probably see those in her nightmares for the rest of her life.

The room began to tilt and swim when Lucy stood. She lost her balance, fell to her knees, and threw up bile, and... were those worms? When she looked again, it was just bile, nothing more.

Lucy gathered her things and turned toward the door to catch sight of a young boy running out of the room and around the corner. She froze, her heart hammering in her chest as adrenaline coursed through her system.

"Jeff?" Her voice was shaky, her throat raw. Lucy tried to say more, but the words wouldn't come to her.

"Lucy?"

The voice came from the hallway. It was distant, quiet, but it was her brother's. Without regard for stealth, Lucy ran out the door and into the hallway. The castle itself was eerily quiet. There should have been screams, gunshots, or at the very least the sound of people running. But the only thing she could hear was her own breathing, and it was the loudest thing in the world at the moment.

"Jeff?"

His name came out as a whisper but still boomed like thunder in her ears. Lucy winced, halfway expecting someone—or that *thing*—to turn the corner and come at her. But there was nothing but silence in response. She crept along the hallway, steeling herself for anything.

When she rounded the corner, Lucy found a bloodstain on the floor leading down the hall and into a slightly ajar door. When her eyes met the doorway, Jeff poked his head out for just a moment, blood still before disappearing back into the darkness.

"Jeff!"

Lucy took off running down the hallway. Her heart hammered in her chest and the exertion caused stars to float in her vision. With wobbly knees and an unsteady gait, Lucy made her way to the door. She knew that Jeff was dead and gone. But after seeing that monstrosity, anything was possible. And even if there was just a small smidgen of hope that she could save Jeff, bring him back and make amends, Lucy had to follow that trail of breadcrumbs all the way to the witch's house, even if there was a hot oven waiting for her.

The door was plain, constructed of cheap wood that looked like it could crack if someone sneezed too hard.

Someone had sneezed too hard.

The door sported a large split, as if someone had shouldered into it. Not only that, but there were bullet holes all throughout. The smell of gunpowder and smoke was thick in the hallway, leaving an almost metallic taste in her mouth.

"Jeff?"

This time when she spoke, it was even quieter, barely perceptible. Lucy still halfway expected a throng of gunfire to explode from inside the room. When nothing happened, she toed the door open, only to find it catching on something heavy on the floor after only an inch or so. She pushed harder, and the door split, cracking like thunder through the hallway and sending her off balance into the dark room.

She landed on something soft and wet. Not the dirt floor she expected. Scrambling to her knees, her hand touched something sticky. Inside the room, the smell of blood was overpowering. Lucy crab walked backward into the hallway and stared at a bloody boot just inside the now broken door.

Light from the hall spilled into the room, which wasn't much bigger than a walk-in closet, exposing a scene that would have put a slaughterhouse to shame. A lone security guard, or rather, what was left of him, lay on the ground. He stared up at the ceiling with wide, dead eyes, both hands on his stomach as he was trying (and failing) to keep his insides from spilling out.

That creature must have gotten to him and split him open. Next to him was a small machine gun, an MP-5. With the door open, the smell was getting even worse, with offal and viscera mixing with the coppery scent. Bile crawled up her throat, and for once she was happy that her stomach was empty.

Lucy grabbed the weapon and checked the magazine. It was empty, but there was a spare on the guard's tactical vest. She grabbed that, racked a round, and put the strap around her neck and shoulder.

A quick search of the man's pockets revealed a wallet, a pocketknife (which she placed in her own pocket), and a set of keys. The lone keychain had a picture of a cartoonish airplane with big eyes and words which read, "I'd rather be flying."

"Trevor! I found them!" Lucy said. "We can get out of he—"

Her stomach growled. The smells of everything were getting to her, but in a different way. Now her mouth watered at the thought of breaking a rib off the guard and sucking the raw meat and juices off of it until it was clean.

Just a taste wouldn't hurt. It might even help center her. Lucy reached out, her fingertips brushing across the edge of a floating rib. It was still a little warm even...

"Lucy?"

The voice came from behind her. She snapped her head around, coming face-to-face with Jeff.

He looked just like she remembered him. Everything was the same, right down to his crappy haircut she had given him with a pair of dull scissors. This time, he didn't have the bloody wound on his head. This time, his presence felt different. Lighter. Warmer.

"Jeff?"

She couldn't help it as the tears burst free. Jeff stared at her with loving eyes and a smile that made her cry even harder.

"Jeff, I am so sorry. You didn't deserve... I wish... I..." her words were lost in a sob that wracked her whole body.

Jeff nodded, smiled, and then disappeared right before her eyes.

When she was done crying, Lucy wiped her face with the grimy sleeve of her coat. The dead guard no longer appealed to her in the slightest, and the fact that she had almost eaten a part of a dead human body was enough to make her shudder.

Lucy pocketed the keys to the plane and went off to find Trevor. They needed to get off the island and away from all the madness before they became a part of it.

Chapter Thirty-Four

Trevor swung the gun in Hank's direction, but Hank was inhumanly fast. And way too accurate for a man without eyes.

Hank slammed into Trevor, slapping the gun out of his hands and grabbing him by the neck. Trevor tried to knock Hank's hand away and break from his grasp, but he would have had better luck trying to bust a 4X4 beam with a broom stick.

Hank smiled, revealing a bloody mouth and teeth that were too long and jagged to be human. He lifted Trevor off the ground until his boots were kicking at Hank's knees.

A guttural bark came from Hank's throat, almost a croak. Then he leaned closer and sniffed Trevor's neck.

"I can smell your meat, your insides, and they smell delectable," Hank said as drool ran from the corners of his mouth. "I'm going to enjoy tearing you apart from the bottom up so you feel every little rip!"

"Y-you don't have to do this," Trevor said, expending what little bit of air he had left. His vision began to tunnel, and he became lightheaded as Hank's grip tightened on his neck.

Hank's grin somehow widened. "I know I don't have to. I want to."

Just as everything was going dark, a low growl came from the doorway. Hank turned his head to look, and that gave Trevor the moment he needed. He slammed both arms down on the crook of Hank's elbow. It wasn't enough to break completely free, but it was enough that he was jostled loose, and blood began to flow through his carotid artery. His vision snapped back into focus, and now he saw what stood at the threshold.

It was the creature.

It angled its massive antlers through the doorway and then stepped through. Hank dropped Trevor, and he crumpled to the ground in a heap, massaging his throat.

"You and I are one!" Hank screamed, opening his arms wide. "We both serve The Devourer!"

The creature sniffed at a dead body and then loped further into the room. It looked at Hank with its head cocked to the side, as if it were really seeing him for the first time.

Then it narrowed its violet eyes, and that low growl came again, so low it rumbled in Trevor's chest. Before Hank could utter another word, the creature pounced, slamming him to the ground. Trevor watched as both monsters battled. Hank was vicious, using everything he could to fight the creature, from his hands to a broken piece of wood from the nearby table.

It was clear who was dominant, and it wasn't Hank. The creature clamped its jaws down on Hank's neck and shook like it was a dog trying to kill a bird or squirrel. Blood, along with bits of flesh and worms, flew across the room like rain. Trevor covered his face with his arm but shivered when globules splattered across his coat.

Seeing that this would be a short fight, Trevor slipped through the door. He closed it behind him and locked it via deadbolt from the other side. It probably wouldn't hold too long against that monster, but a few seconds would be better than nothing.

When he turned, his breath caught in his throat.

He stood at the precipice of a large, circular room made of ancient stone. Thousands of candles sat upon the craggy surface of the wall, along any tiny ledge or outcropping, and illuminated the chamber in a mesmerizing dance of light and shadow. About ten feet into the room, situated in the center, was a giant pit that extended deep into the ground at a sloping angle. It didn't look like any machine had bored such a hole, and it wasn't a natural opening either. No, something had made that. Something living. Something large.

Trevor didn't know how he knew, but the knowledge was stored somewhere deep in his subconscious mind.

That deep dark pit that would stretch on forever to nothing and everything.

To make matters worse, red moss lined the walls of the pit, crawling with more worms. Some of the worms were as thick as baseball bats and garden hoses. But that wasn't the worst of it. It was the bodies.

Dozens upon dozens of bodies of people and animals were caught in the grabbing tendrils. Each body sported uncountable worms boring into their flesh, much like the pit had been bored into the earth.

Those poor souls had been captured, some long ago, based on the style of their clothes, though some wore nothing at all. All of them moved and writhed in pain as the worms dug into their flesh, preserved by some unnatural force. Some even opened their eyes revealing pale white orbs, sucked of all their color, opening their mouths in a silent plea for it all to end.

A group of bodies looked fresh. Still alive and warm. Some wore polo shirts and slacks, like they were retail workers or something. These bodies still fought to get free, though it was a losing battle.

On the other side of the pit was a stone altar decorated with the bones of a creature Trevor couldn't place. Everything about it was abnormally large. It was humanoid, but upon its skull grew massive antlers similar to a stag or elk. Each side sported nearly twenty points, some twisting and curved, others spear like and ready for battle. Standing on the other side of the altar, wearing red robes emblazoned with gold filigree, was Randall King.

"It's beautiful, isn't it?" Randall asked, pointing to the pit. "If you listen closely, you can hear them speak."

Trevor listened. At first, there was nothing. But then, as if someone had flipped a switch, the whispers of those trapped below in the pit crawled into his ears. Not only could he hear them, he could feel their pain, their want and desire for the end, but also something else. A call, a song maybe, sung at the beginning of time when the cosmos was nothing more than a black void where the leviathans swam amongst the darkness looking for something to devour.

Before he knew it, Trevor stood at the edge of the pit. One more step and he'd fall in, joining all those trapped below. He scrambled back and raised his gun, pointing it at Randall.

"Let us go!"

Randall nodded, his smile never faltering even though one squeeze of the trigger and his insides would paint the stone wall behind him.

"Of course, if He wills it, you are free to go. But if He doesn't, then I'm afraid there is nothing I can do."

"Who the fuck are you talking about?" Trevor asked.

"He Who Devours the Stars." Randall placed a hand on the strange skull on the altar and stroked it, as if it were a pet.

"You mean that fucking monster out there?"

Randall laughed, the sound bouncing off the walls. A moment later, a million more voices joined the laugh, all coming from the pit.

"No, not at all. That being is merely an avatar. A righteous claw! An extension of His will."

"You're fucking nuts," Trevor said.

"This has all happened before, and it *will* happen again, my naïve friend. There is nothing you can do to stop it. The cycle will not end until He devours every star in the universe and returns us all to darkness."

"Why are you doing this? Just let us go, or I swear to fuck I will end you now."

Ms. Thomas came out wearing nothing more than a sheer robe the color of lilacs. She stood next to Randall and laid her head on his shoulder.

"We are doing this for knowledge and power," she said.

"It is nearly time, my dear," Randall said as he stepped to the side and waved an arm toward the altar.

Ms. Thomas nodded and used a nearby step stool to step up onto the stone slab. As she did, she let the robe drop, revealing her naked body—a body completely riddled with worms. They crawled just beneath her skin, glowing with violet energy which grew brighter the closer she got to the pit. They writhed with ecstasy, as if in anticipation of what was about to happen.

Something big crashed into the door behind Trevor. It caused dust to fall from the rafters. Two more quick slams hit the door, and he thought it would give way and that monster would come rushing in. But it held.

Ms. Thomas cast a nervous glance toward the noise, but Randall placed a hand on her shoulder, grabbing her attention.

"Can you feel it?" Randall asked her.

She closed her eyes and nodded. "Oh yes, I can feel Him inside me. I can sense his excitement. I can—"

Her face screwed up with pain, cutting her next word short. She tried to say something again, but it only came out as a choked cry. Ms.

Thomas' eyes popped open, no longer full of confidence and smug superiority but fear and agony.

"Wha-, why?" she managed to eke out.

"Because He wills it so. Did you think you were to play a different role in this production?" Randall asked.

Randall raised his arms to the ceiling and began to speak in a language that was guttural and ancient. Trevor had no clue what he was saying but understood what the intent was. This was an offering.

Ms. Thomas screamed, and the wails from the pit echoed her cries. She dropped to her knees, and when she did, a bit of her cheek fell away, revealing a bloody mess of worms beneath. She tried to raise her hand to the new wound, but her fingers sloughed off, replaced by more of the writhing things.

Randall reached a crescendo in his chants and then pushed her body into the pit. Ms. Thomas fell, hitting the edge with a wet slap before rolling into the tunnel. She didn't make it far, as her body caught on some of the red moss. Her cries grew louder as larger worms emerged from the red and bore into her.

A few agonizing seconds later, her cries ceased when one of the worms, the largest Trevor had seen yet, about the size of a mature gator, pushed its way into her back.

"It was her time to join Him," Randall said. Then he turned his attention to Trevor. "And now it is your time."

Chapter Thirty-Five

Randall's eyes radiated with that same infernal violet energy as the rest of the place. The worms in his body took on the same glow, pulsing bright enough to shine through his robes. He leaped through the air, crossing the pit with ease and landing in front of Trevor before he could even squeeze the trigger.

Trevor staggered back, jerking the trigger of the shotgun as he did. The blast hit Randall in the guts, taking a large chunk of ribs and intestine out, but much to Trevor's dismay, Randall only grunted and then smiled.

"He gives me the power to withstand your primitive tools! He gives me the energy to live on! I have endured your pathetic attempts to kill me for thousands of years. I shall endure a millennium more if He wills it so."

As Randall spoke, dozens of the bloody worms crawled out from the wound and started to create a latticework of red moss around it. A heartbeat later, the bleeding stopped, and there was nothing there but a rosy patch of skin.

"What the fuck are you?" Trevor asked.

"Nothing more but a servant in His name."

The thing on the other side of the door bashed against it with renewed fury, the thumps almost in time with the hammering of Trevor's heart.

Yet, the door still held.

Randall rushed forward and hit Trevor in the chest, sending him flying into the nearby wall. Something snapped inside his chest when he hit the wall. There was a sharp pain when he tried to move or breathe, and it was difficult to get a lungful of air.

Randall continued to advance toward him. Trevor pointed the gun at him and quickly shot again. The shotgun blasted Randall in the face, throwing him off balance. But then he turned and looked at Trevor, that evil grin still painted on his mangled face as the worms hurried to repair the damage.

"You cannot kill me," Randall said.

Trevor deflated. He couldn't. Not with the gun or anything else on his person.

He couldn't, but maybe it could.

Trevor pointed the shotgun at the door's lock.

Randall started to run for Trevor. "What are yo—"

The shotgun barked one final time, destroying the lock. In an instant, the door crashed open as the beast lumbered in, ducking to maneuver its antlers through. Blood and gore, along with pieces of Hank's clothing, covered the creature. It looked at Randall.

Randall skidded to a stop and raised his arms wide, hands balled into fists. "I am a servant of He Who Devours the Stars! You will obey me!"

The thing let out a clicking growl that sounded like a tree snapping in half. It took a step forward.

Randall backed up until his heels were at the edge of the pit. The cries from below roared to life with renewed vigor, hungry at the thought of another meal. Trevor swore he could hear Gwendolyn's voice with them this time.

"Stop! I am not the one. It is him!" Randall said, pointing to Trevor. "He wills me to serve!"

The creature, fully in the chamber, stood on its hind legs. Trevor's mind splintered at the sight of it. At that moment, he wished he had saved one shell left for himself.

"I am a faithful servant! I have done His bidding for over two thousand years, and I will not be cowed by the likes of a dog like you!" Randall screamed.

Then it rushed forward, slamming into Randall and goring him through the guts with its antlers. Randall cried out in equal parts pain and frustration as he tried to get free. The creature swung its gaze to Trevor. With its gaze locked on Trevor, it stepped into the pit, taking Randall with it.

A gout of purple flame shot up through the opening of the pit, burning so hot Trevor thought he might combust. The screams of the victims inside joined the inferno. Then, as if someone had flipped a switch, it died down, leaving the room in darkness save the flickering light of a few candles.

For what felt like hours, Trevor lay on the floor staring at the pit. The cries and moans had since stopped, and the room itself was eerily quiet. He kept expecting that thing to come crawling back up and tear him to pieces, but it never did.

Finally, he mustered the strength to get up. When he did, everything hurt, especially his chest. His breath came in ragged wheezes, and he was coughing up bubbly blood. He needed a doctor fast, but sitting on his ass waiting for one wasn't the answer.

He stepped out of the chamber and into the other room to find pieces of Hank *everywhere.* It was impossible to avoid stepping in the bits, so Trevor did his best. When he came into the hall, a familiar voice greeted him.

"Trevor!"

He turned his head, wincing as something shifted inside him. Lucy ran down the hallway and stopped just short of him. A look of concern etched her face.

"What happened?" she asked.

Trevor tried to form the words to answer but just couldn't. He pointed back to the room and when Lucy peered in, her face went pale.

"What in the fuck? You know what, I don't even care anymore. Let's get the hell out of here." Lucy dug the keys out of her pocket and showed them to Trevor.

He gave her a slight smile. The familiar tingle in his stomach appeared at the thought of not only flying again but having to pilot the plane. The last time didn't work out for his father. However, the events of the few hours were enough to push him past that.

They left the building, Lucy helping to support Trevor's weight as he staggered out. Trevor stopped just outside of the plane and put a hand on the fuselage.

Bile crept up his throat, and his breathing, already under a great deal of labor, got even harder. His knees buckled, and Trevor dropped to the ground, tears streaming down his face.

"I can't do this," he whispered, his chest crackling with each word.

Lucy dropped down next to him. "You have to, or we'll both die here."

"I can't. Last time, I—"

Lucy took his face into her hands and looked him in the eyes. "You can. I believe in you. You just survived something so terrifying and crazy it can't be as bad as flying a plane. Please, I don't want to die here, and neither do you."

Trevor didn't know about that. The pain was getting worse now that the adrenaline had worn off. There was something comforting knowing if he just let go and slipped into the void, all that pain would disappear. But then the thought of the pit and what lurked underneath this island crawled into his thoughts. The idea of those worms devouring his corpse was enough to get him moving again.

He nodded and Lucy helped him up and into the plane. After some initial checks and directing Lucy at what needed to happen to get it ready to fly, he fired it up.

Moments later, they were in the air and on their way home.

The initial feeling of dread was still there, like a voice pleading with him to turn around and land, but after a few minutes, it softened. Training took over, and he oriented the plane back toward the mainland and was trying to get someone to respond on the radio.

He was tired. So tired. Perhaps if he just rested his head against the window, he could...

"You did good kid."

Trevor looked over at the passenger seat and didn't find Lucy. Instead, his father sat there with a warm smile on his face.

"Dad?"

His father patted him on the leg, giving it a comforting squeeze. "I'm proud of you. I hope you know that."

Trevor had thought so many times of what he might say if he got to speak to his father again. He'd say how sorry he was and how he wished it had been him who died instead. But now, with his father sitting right next to him, he was speechless.

"It's okay," his father said. Then he nodded toward the horizon. "It's time to fly."

"I love you, Dad."

"I love you too."

Lucy's stomach lurched as the plane dropped in altitude. Trevor slumped over in his seat, chin resting on his chest. She grabbed the controls and did her best to level the plane. She had never flown before, other than playing flight simulators, but managed to at least stop the descent.

"Trevor! Wake up!"

She shook his shoulder, which caused his body to shift. His face and lips were blue, and his skin was very pale. Lucy checked for a pulse but didn't find anything.

"Trevor! Please! Wake up!"

Tears fell down her cheeks as she shook him even harder, but he didn't respond. In the distance, the mainland appeared. She tried to radio for help, but nobody answered. Lucy wasn't even sure if the radio was on or what frequency would work. Not knowing what do, she finally screamed in frustration.

The land came closer and closer, and finally sandy beaches and massive pines loomed in the distance. Below her, fishing and cargo boats cut white trails through the blue sea.

Then, the engine sputtered to stop, and they were gliding.

Lucy found a spot on a nearby beach that looked suitable for landing and veered the plane in that direction. While she didn't know how to fly, she understood the concept enough to know that she had to slow the plane down or they would hit the ground too hard, and nothing would matter after that.

Flaps. She needed to find the flaps. A quick search on the dash and she found a tiny lever that said flaps with an up and a down. The switch was already in the up position. Lucy flipped it down.

The plane slowed. She gradually dropped in altitude the best she could. As she neared the beach, people came into view. Some were pointing and taking video with their cameras, but most were running.

They were the smart ones.

As the ground rushed up to meet her, Lucy dropped the landing gear and closed her eyes, praying to anyone or anything that would listen.

Then, the landing gear touched the sand, and everything went black.

Chapter Thirty-Six

Lucy first came to with a soft beep in her ear. It was rhythmic, almost like a slow metronome. When she opened her eyes, bright light flooded her senses, and she tried to cover her face, only to find her arm encased in something hard.

Finally, her eyes adjusted to the light and her vision returned, although it was somewhat blurry. Bandages or cloth covered one eye, but the other was clear.

She was in a hospital room; her right arm and left leg were in a cast. The television was on but muted, showing an old rerun of *Jeopardy*.

"I'll take surviving the impossible for 1000, Alex," Lucy said to nobody.

A moment later, a Black woman wearing a doctor's white lab coat walked into the room. She had long hair pulled back into a tight bun and wore thick, tortoise-shell glasses that fell to the edge of her nose. When she looked up from her clipboard and saw Lucy, she pushed the glasses up onto the bridge of her nose and smiled.

"Finally awake, I see," the woman said.

"Where am I?"

Lucy's throat was dry and raw. She needed water and food.

"You're at Mercy's Rest Hospital in Rimshaw, Oregon. You're lucky to be alive and—for the most part—in one piece, Ms. Bingham. I'm Dr. Madeline Grace."

Lucy tried to sit up and scratch her face with her other arm, but when she moved, something stopped her after just a few inches. A metal set of handcuffs secured her arm to the bed's frame.

"Just a precaution. There are some detectives that would love to ask you some questions about why you crash landed on the beach."

"Where's Trevor?" Lucy asked, looking around the room.

The doctor's smile disappeared. "I'm afraid your friend didn't make it. If it is any consolation, he was dead before you hit the ground. Blood loss and a punctured lung."

Lucy let herself sink into the bed. She wanted to cry. She wanted to scream. But most of all, she wanted to get out of the hospital.

"Get me out of these things," she said and tugged her arm against the cuffs.

"I'm afraid I can't do that. But I'll let the detectives know you are awake. I'm sure they'll be by later this afternoon to speak with you. How are you feeling?"

Lucy sighed, trying the cuffs one more time. She lay her head against the pillow and closed her eyes. Her body hurt, but overall, it didn't feel as bad as she thought it would. In fact, Lucy felt more pain when she pinched a nerve in her neck a few years back.

"I'm feeling fine, really. Just thirsty. And hungry."

"That great! Even if the detectives say you're free to leave, we'll need to keep you here for another night or two for observation. You hit your head quite hard in the landing. But I'll see if I can get the nurse to bring you some lunch from the cafeteria."

At the thought, her stomach growled.

Lucy hoped they were serving meat...

Acknowledgements

Creating a book is not a solo endeavor. Of course I had to write it myself, but there have been so many folks out there that have had a hand in helping me create this story. First off, tremendous shout out to my spouse, Jennifer. Her support allowed me to spend time on this project. Next, thank you Michael Knost for early developmental edits. Thank you to Stacey Kondla and her team for helping take this story in the direction it needed to go. Without her support and suggestions, this book would have turned out a lot differently. A huge high five to Don Noble for bringing my ideas for the cover to life! I would be remiss not to send thanks to Beverly Bernard for her awesome editing. Also, thank you Caryn Larrinaga and Peggy Reed for beta reading this along the journey and giving me valuable feedback.

And, of course, thank you my amazing readers. Without you, this would never exist in the first place.

-C.R. Langille

About the Author

C.R. Langille spent many a Saturday afternoon watching monster movies with her mom, a tradition that would eventually lead a queer, transgender woman to find her voice as an award-winning horror author. Langille is the founder of Timber Ghost Press, holds an MFA: Writing Popular Fiction from Seton Hill University, is an affiliate member of the Horror Writers Association, and serves as the DEI Chair for the League of Utah Writers where she was also named Editor of the Year in 2024.

A Note from Timber Ghost Press

If you enjoyed *The Worms Shall Feast,* please consider leaving a review on Amazon or Goodreads. Reviews help the authors and the press.

If you go to www.timberghostpress.com you can sign up for our newsletter so you can stay up-to-date on all our upcoming titles, plus you'll get informed of new horror flash fiction and poetry featured on our site monthly.

Take care and thanks for reading *The Worms Shall Feast!*

-Timber Ghost Press

www.ingramcontent.com/pod-product-compliance
Lightning Source LLC
LaVergne TN
LVHW090600110826
845146LV00001B/208

* 9 7 9 8 9 9 2 5 7 6 7 4 0 *